His Second Chance

Mary Walsh

His Second Chance

Copyright
Published by Mary Walsh
©2020 Mary Walsh

All rights reserved
marywalshwrites.com

No part of this publication may be reproduced or distributed in print or electronic form without prior permission from the author.

His Second Chance

Discover other books by Mary Walsh

The Curse of Jean Lafitte
Knights of the Corporate Round Table
American Posse
Memories of 9/11
Plenty of Fish in the Ocean State
Once Upon a Time in Chicago
Wounded but not Dead
Where or When
Fine Spirits Served Here
Life Lessons for my Kids
You Deserve Better
Stable of Studs
Dragon Slayer
Catch a Break

His Second Chance

His Second Chance

Chapter 1

BANG!

"What the hell was that?" I exclaimed to my buddy Prashant. He and I had been working nonstop for the past five days in the chemistry lab at Carnegie Mellon University in Pittsburgh. He was a Ph.D. candidate and he needed a couple of extra hands to help him create a new lithium-ion battery to extend the life of cell phones. I took a week off on a staycation from my consulting job at Deloitte to help him out.

While I examined the electrical charge control, he tested the bimetal thermal cutoffs. Earlier in the week, we successfully merged the components to create a three-day battery. But Prashant had always been an overachiever. He wanted a battery to last seven days before it needed to be charged again.

Exhausted, I couldn't remember the last time I took a shower, let alone ate something. A couple of dozen empty cans of Red Bull

His Second Chance

were scattered around the floor. Songs from Guns N' Roses and Aerosmith blasted through Prashant's iPhone. I wasn't used to this kind of schedule, but boy did it bring me back to the good old days where we'd push through 50-60 hours of work at a time, stopping only for pizza, chips, and soda to keep our geek quest alive. I was getting too old for this shit.

We gaped over to the heat sealer where hydrofluoric acid and lithium hydroxide had been pressurizing for the past hour. I remembered locking the lid, but something gurgled inside. We both glared at it in anticipation, unsure if we should grab a fire extinguisher or not.

"I don't know, man," Prashant replied, his dark hair stood out on ends in an aimless array as if he'd stuck a fork into an electric socket. His rumpled and stain-filled maroon CMU hoodie had seen better days. A dark half-inch beard covered his face because he hadn't shaved in over a week. "I thought you sealed it?"

"I did," I countered, rubbing a palm along my own stubble-laden jaw. "I'm sure I did."

Uneasy, we inched over to the edge of the metal table, curious of what could be happening on the inside of the wide ceramic cylinder.

BANG!

"What the hell—" I gasped, eyeballing the heat sealer.

BANG! BANG! BANG! BANG! BANG!

His Second Chance

Prashant and I ran for cover under the metal tables as the cylinder exploded, sending emission particles all over the small room. White sparks showered down, igniting small puffs of fireballs into the air. Each fireball turned blue, then purple, then red, and extinguished within a few seconds before sizzling ash fell to the floor. A fizzing sound accompanied each one. The room echoed like our own personal Independence Day celebration.

After a few minutes, the shower of fireballs stopped and the room was silent. Prashant and I glanced at each other under the table as if to say, *Do you think it's safe to come out now?*

I took the lead and slowly slinked upward and trekked a few steps, my eyes focused on the cauterized cylinder. Prashant stayed behind me, under the table. A few of the burned-out fireballs caused singe marks on the computer monitors and keyboard in front of me. The Q button was missing. Didn't have much use for it anyway.

"Is it over?" Prashant called to me from under the table.

"Yes, I think—"

KABOOM!

The last thing I remembered was the blast knocking me off my feet and my body thumping on the floor.

"Ryan!" Prashant knelt over me and slapped my face a few times. His knee jabbed into my side and I coughed. "Ryan! Are you okay?"

His Second Chance

On the floor, I blinked a few times and raised a hand to my cheek where he smacked me. He had pushed up the sleeves of his hoodie to reveal the black tattoo on his forearm.

"Yeah, I'm okay," I sputtered in between sharp breaths. "Dude, get your knee out of my ribs."

"Oh, sorry." Prashant shifted his body to give me more space on the linoleum next to him.

"What happened?" I grunted, trying to sit up. A noxious haze of smoke covered the lab, but nothing was on fire. I raked a hand through my brown hair that had been slowly inching backward over the years.

"I don't know, man," Prashant replied. "I thought we had all of our calculations right, but something exploded inside." He studied my limp body again. "Maybe you should see a doctor? There's an urgent care a coupla blocks away."

"I think I'll be okay." I gingerly eased myself up to a sitting position. "Besides, you need me for a few more days."

"If you say so," Prashant said. Through the smoke, Prashant admired his work around the room from where we hunkered on the floor. "It's pretty cool, isn't it? Even the explosion is cool. If you would have stayed on the long and scholarly road with me, you could have been working with me every day instead of bitching about traveling all the time."

Prashant had a point. Being a Consulting Manager on the road for Deloitte took its toll on me. I'd spend one week in Dallas, the next in Minneapolis, the next in Boston. I constantly lived out of a suitcase and barely had time for myself. Being on the road so much

His Second Chance

prevented me from dating or even making a good meal in my own kitchen. The money and lifestyle appealed to me, as compared to staying in Pittsburgh with Prashant and hacking computer code in a cubicle somewhere for a fraction of what I'd make on the West Coast. I earned a lot of money, but with such a travel-heavy lifestyle, I had no one to spend it with. A while back, I dated a woman named Rebecca for several years but she eventually grew tired of my vagabond lifestyle and broke up with me. Last I heard, she married a middle-school teacher, had two kids, and lived on the outskirts of D.C. I loved Rebecca but I could never bring myself to make a real commitment with her.

Admittedly, I was a little jealous of Prashant. He and his wife, Manju, lived in a restored, brick-row home a mile from CMU campus in North Oakland. He bragged that he could bike to work and grow organic vegetables in a garden. They chased their kids around in nearby Schenley Park. They had their pick of restaurants they could walk to. They made friends with their neighbors. He could have buddies like me stay with him. I envied his simple lifestyle, even in the rare times like this where he spent time at the lab and didn't get to spend dinners with his family for a week.

"We had some awesome times together, didn't we?" I reminisced.

"Yeah, we did." Prashant stood, then offered his hand to me to pull me off the floor. "You can help me out anytime, brother."

I dusted deviated soot from my sweatshirt and flicked it to the ground. As I took my first step, a jolt of pain rushed up my back.

Shrieking out, I hunched over in agony, seeking support from the metal lab table.

"Dude, you need to go lay down," Prashant told me. "Manju's home with the kids. Ask her to get you an ice pack and some Tylenol." He pulled his cell phone out of his pocket and quickly tapped it. "I'll get you an Uber, then I'll clean up this mess. I should go home to my kids for a few days anyways. They probably forgot what I look like."

"Thanks, man," I said through gritted teeth. I gripped the table with all my might as another jolt of pain cursed through my back. "I appreciate you letting me bunk with you."

"Of course. You always have a place to stay with us." Prashant stepped over to me, slung my left arm around his neck, put his right arm around my back, and helped me walk out the door to the waiting Uber. I couldn't ask for a better friend.

* * * *

After two days of resting my back on Prashant and Manju's couch watching cartoons with their young kids Taj and Gia, I longed to be vertical again. Yellow and blue blobs bouncing and singing across the TV screen were enough to get me motivated. I didn't understand how parents of grade school kids could stand watching that chaotic kaleidoscope without drinking a couple of beers. Or maybe they did?

I shuffled into the kitchen and found Prashant and Manju at the table with an open laptop in front of them. Small-scale

His Second Chance

backpacks scattered on the floor, spilling colorful papers and crayons into a small mound. A large print of the Hyderabad temples hung on the opposite, spotless, white wall of the kitchen.

Prashant and Manju stopped what they were doing and glared up at me.

"Look who's up and moving around," Manju joked.

Out of habit, I ran my fingers along a two-inch scar across the webbed section of my right hand between my thumb and forefinger. Sometimes I didn't even realize I did it. A few months after Prashant and Manju got married, I was in their kitchen slicing a bagel with a filet knife. My left hand slipped and sliced my right, sending blood everywhere. Quick thinking, Manju wrapped my hand in a fat gauze and brought me to the ER. The scar reminded me that being a knife thrower was not in my future.

"I see you're still rubbing that thing." Manju eyed me. "Next time you'll remember not to cut a bagel with a fish knife."

"I can't help it your knives aren't left-handed," I joked.

"Not like those green-handled scissors in elementary school, right?" Manju parried.

"What do you two want for dinner tonight?" I asked them, dodging her jab. She and I parried like brother and sister taking fun potshots at each other. "My treat for taking care of me for the past two days."

Prashant and Manju glanced at each other and then back at me. "Hemingway's has the best burgers. It's up on Forbes Avenue right next to the Towers," Prashant said. "The kids will eat them, too.

HIS SECOND CHANCE

They can share one." He picked up a stray action figure from the table and tossed it into a nearby toy box on the floor. "Thank you."

"And get French fries, too," Manju added. She pushed a rogue strand of her long dark hair behind her ear. I guessed the stress and energy it took chasing after young kids and working a full-time job zapped the life out of her.

"But you guys don't eat beef?" I glared at them.

"Only on Mondays." Prashant barked a laugh and raised an upward finger to his lips. "Shhh, don't tell my parents." Prashant's mom and dad had immigrated from India to the States in the 70s and still maintained their firm traditions. Much to his parents' chagrin, Prashant declined an arranged marriage, but they were placated by the fact that Manju was Indian as well. They would have died an early death and haunted him from the grave if he had married a white girl.

"You two are so good together," I told them. "Prashant, you found your soulmate in that girl. You lucky bastard."

"Yes, he is." Manju kissed her husband on the mouth. "And, fortunately for me, good thing you dated that girl Devya your freshman year well before you met me, otherwise I would've been the first girl you kissed, too."

Prashant's mouth fell open. "Manju! I never told Ryan that! Or any of the other guys we hung with for that matter."

"So, you're saying you didn't kiss a girl until you were in college?" I pondered.

Prashant huffed and lowered his head. "Yes."

HIS SECOND CHANCE

"Good thing we didn't know," I said. "Otherwise, we would've ragged on you for years!"

"I know." Prashant chuckled. "Why do you think I didn't tell any of you numbnuts?"

Fifteen minutes later, I stood at the take-out counter in Hemingway's Cafe. A giant sign promoting $5.50 Bud Light pitchers swung from the ceiling above me. Voted the best college bar in the 'Burgh, Hemingway's was peaceful now as I waited on four burgers and orders of fries for dinner from the kitchen staff. Droves of college students from Carnegie Mellon, University of Pittsburgh, and Carlow University would come later tonight to sing karaoke, dance, and down cheap beer.

I rested my arms on the counter in front of me. The shiny, lacquered bar embalmed once-used beer bottle caps in a grid pattern as far as I could see. Corona. Heineken. MGD. Budweiser. Miller Lite. Did someone spend hours painstakingly placing each bottle cap in a perfect grid? Someone with a lot of time on their hands.

"Do you want a drink while you wait?" the bartender asked me. She wore a tight black tank top emblazoned with *Lite* across her ample chest. The college boys loved her and constantly hit on her. I caught myself staring at her a few times, even though she was a good fifteen years younger than me.

"Yeah, do you have any Red Bull?" I asked her. "Give me two, if you have 'em."

"Sure." She turned around and opened a glass-faced refrigerator, grabbed two large cans of Red Bull, and set them on the bar in front of me.

His Second Chance

"Thanks." I cracked one open and gulped half the can.

A few minutes later, the young, cute bartender placed the bill and two white plastic bags full of food containers in front of me. "That'll be $53.50."

I pulled a credit card out of my wallet and handed it to her. As she rang up my tab, I clattered the empty can of Red Bull on the bar in front of me.

Moments later, I stepped outside on the sidewalk of busy Forbes Avenue. Affectionately known as "The Towers," the three-building, 20-story Litchfield Towers Pitt dorms hovered above me to the left. Rumor was they were tiny dorm rooms reminiscent of prison cells, but they had been there as long as I could remember. Cars, buses, and bicycles whizzed along Forbes in front of me. Anyone who dared to cross the three-lane boulevard without the security of the neon walk sign took their life in their hands.

As I took a few steps up the sidewalk toward my rental car, the street lamp above me exploded, sending a small shower of sparks and broken pieces of bulbs on top of me.

"Holy shit!" I said to myself, trying to cover my head in vain with the bags of food.

Relieved that I didn't encounter the same fate from the lab a few days earlier, I made my way to my car and drove back to Prashant and Manju's house.

His Second Chance

Chapter 2

The next morning, I woke up to the sound of horns blaring on the street outside. The sun hadn't risen yet, so I blindly searched with my hands along the wall of the first-floor guest bedroom for a light switch. Since it was a Saturday, Prashant, Manju, and their kids were all still sleeping on the second floor. I could make myself some coffee in the kitchen without disturbing them.

I flipped the switch on and covered my eyes from the glaring overhead light. Instead of seeing Manju's good taste in dark dressers with silver accents and luscious linens, a mattress lay on the floor with mismatched sheets, and two hand-me-down dressers filled in the corners of the room. Dark blue, light-blocking curtains covered the windows. Christmas lights hung around the frames.

Where was I?

Was I still dreaming?

I picked up a crisp, new *Sports Illustrated* magazine from one of the dressers. Bobby Hurley was on the cover for Duke winning

His Second Chance

back-to-back NCAA basketball championships -- in 1992. Strange. The mailing label displayed my name and college address. I recalled that my parents bought me a subscription my junior year so that I would have regular mail coming in, even though sports wasn't my thing. Despite my parents' best efforts, the only issue I cared about was the swimsuit edition. Once I started traveling for Deloitte and wasn't home as much, I stopped the subscription.

Things made total sense. I was dreaming about being in college again. I still had a few more hours until I needed to wake up and spend the day with Prashant and his family until I had to catch a plane the next morning. My next work assignment was in Sacramento.

"Ryan?" Someone called me from the other side of the bedroom door. The voice sounded familiar, but it was too muffled for me to recognize who spoke.

"Ryan, you in there?" the voice yelled again. "Phone call."

A phone call? Who had a landline anymore? Why wasn't the person calling my cell? I aimlessly patted the pockets of my jeans and came up empty. Where was my cell phone? Of course. I might not have a cell phone in my dreams. That explained it.

A knock came from the other side of the bedroom door.

I opened the door to Prashant. He wore holey jeans; a long-sleeved, blue T-shirt; and a grey, short-sleeved, Eric Clapton concert T-shirt over top of it. His hair was trimmed and combed down in a neat part. He wore round, wire-framed eyeglasses that had a few kinks in them. His baby-faced cheeks bore a few stubbles but he wouldn't need to shave for another week.

His Second Chance

I gaped at him. He appeared nothing like he did the previous night when we noshed on burgers and fries with his wife and kids. Last night, he dressed like a mid-forties dad who didn't get enough sleep. Now he would get carded for buying beer.

"Dude, I called you two times now," Prashant said, obviously annoyed that he was my answering service. "What're you doing in there? Rubbing one out? Let's go. Maggie's on the phone." He turned and walked down the hall.

Maggie.

Oh my god. Maggie.

Maggie and I had our first date in the fall of my sophomore year at Carnegie Mellon. She came to campus then to visit her brother Kevin, who lived next door to me in the dorm. She was a freshman at the University of Pennsylvania in Philadelphia and was home on fall break visiting their parents who lived in the suburbs. I remembered seeing her the first time freshman year when she came to check out a few classes with Kevin at CMU before deciding on Penn. She sat with her brother in the back of the classroom but didn't say much. After that, the other guys on the floor and I constantly teased Kevin about how hot his sister was. Early sophomore year, I finally convinced Kevin to set me up with her. After that serendipitous arranged meeting, I was smitten. Maggie brought a spark to my life and I constantly told myself, "Wow, I like her. I want her".

Maggie and I dated on and off for three years. She was fun, smart, and super hot. I could tell her anything and never feel

HIS SECOND CHANCE

insecure or awkward. My heart thumped out of my chest—she made me believe that I was the only person in the room.

One morning after she spent the night, the scent of her shampoo lingered on my pillow. The enchanting fragrance stayed for a couple of days, reminding me how amazing she was.

My buddies always ragged on me that Maggie was way out of my league. What she saw in an awkward nerd like me, I never comprehended. She constantly told me she liked me and provided me with a huge ego boost. I adored her, but the cross-state distance made an exclusive relationship difficult and we drifted apart, though I never forgot her.

After graduation, I found out through Kevin that Maggie married some guy from her college. Admittedly, I was jealous. Maggie and I reconnected online a few years later and stayed in touch through the decades. She'd tell me about her job, her family, and her adventures in Philly. I'd tell her about traveling for work and the pitfalls of dating in my 30s and 40s. We talked like best friends, spilling secrets that we knew no one else would understand.

One night, when I was in Philadelphia for work several years after she graduated, Maggie and I met for dinner and drinks. I was nervous as hell to see her, but everything calmed down when she arrived at my hotel to pick me up. She looked gorgeous. Her long, leather coat and sexy heels with dark tights made me wonder if they were thigh-high. After several hours of natural conversation, I leaned in for a requisite goodbye hug; our lips were so close and I kissed her. Fireworks went off in my brain as her soft warm mouth covered mine in an achingly familiar way. No one ever kissed as well as the

His Second Chance

two of us. She broke off the kiss and turned me down, talking about her loyalties to her significant other. The guy she was with couldn't be as good as me, but I couldn't offer her anything consistent. She deserved better than me.

I ran into her again a few years later when Kevin got married. Jealousy, and several shots of tequila, surged through me that night while I stared at her dancing the night away with her husband. Later that night, I stared at the ceiling of my hotel room wishing circumstances were different. If I only had another chance with her.

Maggie was always the one who got away. I cursed myself every day for letting her go. No matter how hard I tried, I couldn't quit her. I never failed at anything, but I felt like I failed to move on with my life. I thought about her every day even though we had both taken different directions. But maybe I wasn't *supposed* to quit her?

As I left the college bedroom to get the phone somewhere down the hall, I caught a glimpse of myself in the bathroom mirror and stopped cold. My wavy, dark brown hair hadn't been cut in a few months and reached the tip of my nose. Not that I was heavy in my 40s, but I was now much thinner. Too thin. I wore a rumpled, maroon CMU sweatshirt that I swore I lent to my brother after graduation and he never returned it.

Where was I?

Chapter 3

"Hi Ryan!" Maggie beamed into the phone. "I'm still in Philly. My train is a half-hour late. It says I'll be there by 8:30, but it's anyone's guess with Amtrak."

"What?" I blinked in stupefaction. Annoyed, I hunched over the make-shift phone station in the hallway. The push-button phone sat atop a thick phone book on top of a wooden stool. The short cord tethered me to a two-foot radius.

"I said I'm still in Philly and my train is running behind," she repeated. "I arrived at the station early and found out the train is late anyway. So, I have to stay and wait for it."

"What time is it?" I asked, more wanting to know for myself than for her.

"It's almost 11:30," she said.

"In the morning?" I gasped. The light-blocking curtains in my room gave me no sense of time earlier.

His Second Chance

"Yes, in the morning," Maggie answered. "Ryan, are you okay? What's wrong? Do you still want me to come visit for the weekend or what? You're acting weird."

"Yes, yes, of course I want to see you." I rubbed a hand along my stubbled jaw. The last thing that I remembered was eating burgers with Prashant and Manju. Now I was in my apartment of my junior year of college. I had to be dreaming. I had to be.

"So, I'll meet you at the train station?" Maggie confirmed.

"Yeah, I'll be there."

"Okay, see you tonight," Maggie cooed into the phone.

"See you then," I said.

After I hung up and put the phone back on its base, I wandered down the short hallway toward the kitchen. Prashant stood in the small beige room making himself a peanut butter sandwich.

"Dude, you look like hell." He sniffed me as if I hadn't showered in days.

"I... I... What?" I muttered.

"You okay, man?" Prashant questioned. "Did you drink too much last night? Did someone slip you somethin'?"

"The only thing I remember drinking was Red Bull," I told him.

"What's red bull?" he asked. "Some weird Spanish drink?"

"Huh?" I stared blankly at him.

"Whatever, man." Prashant brushed me off and focused on slapping his sandwich with gobs of peanut butter. "My car keys are in the top drawer over there."

His Second Chance

"Why do I need your car keys?" I wondered. Where was my rental car?

"You know, to pick up Maggie tonight," he explained, glaring back at me. "You can't possibly *walk* four miles to the train station. It's all the way down by the Convention Center. She'd kill you if she had to trek all the way back here."

I blankly stared at him.

"Are you high or something, man? What the hell?" Prashant asked me. "You're acting weird. Weirder than normal." Admittedly, I was OCD in college. Prashant and Kevin made fun of my color-coded closet and my sharpening of my pencils to a perfect point. In my 40s, I had graduated from wooden pencils to a pristine iPad, but my closet was still in rainbow order.

"What? No. You know I don't do drugs," I replied. At least not the hard stuff. Prashant and I occasionally smoked weed, but that was reserved for special occasions.

Kevin wandered into the kitchen, interrupting us.

"I banged on your door," he explained, "but no one answered. I heard you guys in here, so I let myself in."

Maggie's brother and I had lived next door to each other in our freshman dorm and we became fast friends. Like Prashant, he appeared to be 21 years old. His shaggy blonde hair reached the crests of his shoulders, prompting his mother's nagging to get it cut. I gawked at him, studying his youthful looks and baby-faced cheeks. He wore faded jeans and a wrinkled, dark green T-shirt that he picked up from the floor. If I remembered correctly, Kevin wasn't the clothes-hound like I was.

His Second Chance

Kevin tapped his watch.

"Come on, we're gonna be late to class," he said.

I continued to stare at him without moving or speaking.

"Something wrong with him?" Kevin asked Prashant while nodding toward me.

"I dunno," Prashant answered. "He's been acting weird for the past half hour. Ever since Maggie called."

"He was fine yesterday," Kevin carried on the conversation about me as if I wasn't even in the room. "What happened with Maggie?"

"No clue," Prashant replied. "He said something about a red bull. Do you know what that is?"

"Nope," Kevin said, turning, reversing his steps. "Let's go."

In a trance, I grabbed my backpack from the floor and followed the guys out the door to class.

We shuffled down Beeler Street toward campus, passing students on bikes, groups of other guys heading to class, and a few cars. Tall oak trees shaded Beeler Street, giving it a residential feel even though college students rented most of the older red brick homes. Telephone wires stretched across the road. A graffiti-splattered public mailbox stood sentry at the intersection that bordered campus.

A few minutes later, we settled into seats for our Advanced Algorithms class. Every student around me resembled an early 90s grunge model. They wore baggy jeans, plaid flannels, and dark T-shirts. Even the few girls in the class. Most of the students wore lanyards around their necks that held IDs and keys.

His Second Chance

I was having a trippy dream. Maybe Prashant was right? Maybe someone slipped me something in the Red Bull?

For the rest of the day, I trailed Kevin and Prashant around campus. We ran in to other friends on the quad, grabbed a slice of pizza at Skibo Cafe, and split up when Prashant and I headed to Chem lab and Kevin wandered off to his Mechanical Engineering class. Even though I majored in Math, I still needed Chemistry credits to graduate. I had forgone Mechanical Engineering with Kevin because it ate a class slot and I didn't want to study those two semesters of physics or one semester of honors Chem. Even though Kevin was in the Mech E class and could have helped me out, his high As made him a curve-breaker. What a prick.

After the three-hour lab, Prashant and I trekked back to our apartment. The sun had started to set as we wandered down Beeler Street, pushing hues of orange, yellow, and purple at us.

"Ryan, you sure you're okay?" Prashant asked me.

"Yeah, why?" I answered in a sing-song voice. This dream was pretty cool. I was reliving a lot of awesome times of my younger self. I sniffed the air trying to inhale a whiff of second-hand weed somewhere. That would've been a bonus.

"You're acting strange today. You barely said anything in class and you've been staring at me like I have three heads," Prashant replied.

"I'm fine. I swear."

When we approached the front door, Prashant unlooped the lanyard from his neck and pinched his key between his fingers, aiming to match the key to the lock.

His Second Chance

He unlocked the door with his key and I followed him inside. We stepped into the front room that housed a couple of mismatched sofas and a tattered, overstuffed chair. We used a weathered vintage trunk for a coffee table. My mother's old, gold, velvet curtains hung from curtain rods above the windows. A gigantic console TV took up the entire space of a bricked-in fireplace. I couldn't remember the last time I saw a TV that thick and heavy.

Prashant dropped his backpack on the floor along the wall, then headed toward the kitchen.

"Do you want to order something to eat with me?" he asked me while perusing a few take-out menus. "Or are you getting something later with Maggie?"

"Umm..."

"Maggie will be hungry when she gets here," Prashant decided for me. "You'd better wait to eat with her. She got pretty testy with me the last time. As soon as you fed her, she was fine." He pulled the phone off the wall hook and dialed a number. Another landline phone. I was definitely dreaming.

Twenty minutes later, someone knocked on our door as we watched TV.

"My sub's here." Prashant jumped up from the couch, ambled toward the front door, and opened it.

"That'll be $8.50," the exhausted delivery boy told him. He held a crumpled brown paper bag in his hand.

Prashant pulled his wallet out of his back pocket, opened it, and paused. He glanced at the delivery guy, then to me sitting on the couch, then back to the delivery guy.

His Second Chance

"Ryan, do you have any ones?" he asked me. "I only have a ten. I have enough for the sandwich but not much for a tip. Can you spot me a dollar?"

"Sure," I said, hopping up from the sofa and reaching in my pocket at the same time. I handed him a crumpled single. He handed it to the delivery guy along with his ten in exchange for the brown bag of food. The delivery guy turned away and Prashant shut the door. "Why didn't you use Grubhub? You can add the tip on that."

"What's Grubhub?" Prashant gave me another funny look. I lost count how many times he gawked at me like that today.

"You know," I explained, "the app on your phone? You aren't this thick. You use it all the time."

"Dude, there's nothing on my phone except the antenna." Prashant pointed to the cordless phone snuggled in its base on the wall ten feet away from us. He shook his head at me. "What's wrong with you today? Maybe you need to get laid. And that's on Maggie."

He bunched the sack of food in his hand and trotted off to the kitchen for a drink.

I stood there with my hands out, dumbfounded. "What just happened?" I said to myself. "Did I miss something?"

At 8:00, Prashant tossed me his car keys. "Go easy on the clutch this time. Tell Maggie I'll catch her in the morning. I'm heading out to the ATO party."

"Thanks, I will," I replied. I studied the metal keys in my hand. No keyless remote. The keychain had a Saab logo on it.

HIS SECOND CHANCE

I headed out the door and searched for the vehicle parked on the street. Fortunately, Prashant's red Saab 900 stood out pretty well among the other black and grey cars along the road. If I was dreaming, how could I visualize color?

I unlocked the car door with the key and hopped in. I hadn't driven a stick shift in years. No Bluetooth or rear camera. The car didn't even have a CD player. Lots of black knobs and fat buttons across the dashboard to adjust the radio and temperature. Driving old-school was an understatement.

Once I put my foot on the clutch, I turned the engine over with deftness. I shifted the car into reverse and eased off the clutch while I slowly accelerated the gas. Ka-thunk. Damn, I stalled it. Good thing Prashant wasn't with me; he'd make fun of me. I turned the engine again and it purred like a kitten.

I slid out of the parking spot and cruised down Beeler Street, successfully shifting into second and then to third.

Chapter 4

At 8:20, I pulled into the narrow parking lot at the train station. Above me, the interstate overpass rumbled with cars. A couple of Greyhound buses rolled by heading to the nearby bus station. Train whistles and warning sirens sounded off. The newer entrance to the Amtrak station wilted in comparison to the old, opulent Union Station that had been converted to luxury apartments in the late 80s. The Grand Hall of the old station featured arched openings, marble floors, ornate walls, and 40-foot vaulted ceilings with skylights. Checking across the street at the convention center, the old structure amazed me. I was pretty impressed to have this level of detail in my dream!

I parked Prashant's Saab, leaving it in first gear, climbed out, and locked it up. Even though the sky was dark, the air was comfortable and dry. My sweatshirt was enough to keep me warm.

As I wandered into the train station hub, small groups of people exited, dodging me. A large board in the center of the room displayed arrival and departure times. Maggie's train was three minutes away.

The large room bustled with hordes of people. Some folks held their luggage nearby waiting to board their train. Others held signs and flowers, anticipating the return of their friends and family. Darn, I should have bought flowers for Maggie. She loved tulips.

Exhausted Amtrak employees called out directions, anxious for the day to be over. "The 43 Pennsylvanian is arriving on track two," a crackled voice on a loudspeaker announced. Maggie's train. I couldn't wait to see her. My heart jumped in double-time.

I darted across the large room, closer to the gate for track two, winding my way around other people. My cheeks burned with joy.

A few travelers lugging suitcases entered the waiting area. Then a few more. And a few more. Where was Maggie?

I shuffled my feet in place, shifting my weight in anticipation. Whenever I spent time with her, I was a mess. She took my breath away. Even after all this time, I was just as nervous as the first day I met her. She made me weak and strong at the same time.

Maggie finally came into view, dragging a small suitcase behind her. Wow, she was stunning. Her long blonde hair fell down her back into golden strands. She wore tight, faded jeans that hugged her luscious curves. An unzipped, short, black leather jacket covered her white T-shirt. Her green eyes found mine and she flashed a wide, toothy grin at me. She appeared young and fresh, not a wrinkle or a grey hair on her. I rushed over to her.

His Second Chance

"You're here!" I gushed to her. Simultaneously, I grabbed her bag and kissed her on the mouth, enveloping her with my free hand. Her tiny body molded into mine. "It's been so long."

"You saw me last month," she chuckled. "For spring break, remember?"

"Are you hungry?" I asked her, escorting her down the hallway. I held her hand in mine. Her soft palm fit warm and snugly into mine, like the two halves of yin and yang. I had ached with longing for this feeling. Years had passed since the last time we touched like this.

"Yes, famished," she answered. "The dining car was closed so I haven't eaten anything since I left Philly."

"There's a taco place right up the street we can go to," I told her. "It's a five-minute walk."

"I don't care," she groaned. "I'm starving."

After we dropped Maggie's bag at the car, we headed to the taco joint. Other patrons sparsely filled the counter-service eatery, late for the dinner rush and early for the late-night eaters after they hit a few bars. Colorful framed mirrors hung from the walls. Salsa music complemented the atmosphere.

At the counter, I ordered a handful of tacos for us to share and a couple of large sodas. With a tray in my hands, I followed Maggie to a corner booth. I couldn't take my eyes off her magnificent ass. How she kept it in such great shape after all these years was beyond me!

"What are we doing after this?" Maggie asked me, taking a bite of her taco.

His Second Chance

"I don't know." I slurped a big gulp of my soda. "What do you want to do?"

"Well, what's Prashant doing?" she inquired.

"He said something about heading to an ATO party," I replied, taking another long drink.

"Oh yeah, his frat party," Maggie said. "Let's go there."

"Sure, whatever you want, babe." I didn't care where Maggie wanted to go, as long as I was with her. I'd crawl in a hole with her. (She'd even be able to convince me to listen to opera. I was far from an opera fan.) Better take her to a party where I had my name on the standing guest list and could soak in the satisfaction of seeing my girl get hit on by an endless stream of fraternity guys.

Twenty minutes later, we finished our tacos and sodas and hopped into Prashant's car.

As I put the Saab in gear and turned the key, the engine rolled over, puffing out a loud rumbling sound. The car weirdly coughed and then died.

"Don't you know how to drive this?" Maggie laughed at me.

"Yes, of course, I do." I turned my head to the left, away from her, so she couldn't see my crimson cheeks.

Once I turned the engine, we cruised along the Boulevard of the Allies, the Monongahela River shimmered from the illuminated downtown buildings on our right.

Ten minutes later, we rumbled up Beeler Street and found street parking a few spots down from my place.

His Second Chance

As we exited the car, I grabbed Maggie's bag from the trunk. As she stood beside me next to the car, she pushed her sleeve back on her left hand and huffed.

"Crap, I forgot my watch. I'm surprised I made it on time to class this morning."

"I have mine on." I let go of Maggie's suitcase for a moment and inched back the cuff on my right hand. "It's almost 10."

"I sometimes forget that you're left-handed," she said.

"That's why I always sit on the left side of you," I told her. "Did you never realize that?"

"Oh, right." She beamed at me with sparkling, jade eyes. I could get lost in those eyes.

"Can we go watch a movie tomorrow?" Maggie batted her eyelashes at me. "I haven't had a chance to see it yet."

"Of course, whatever you want," I said. "What movie?"

"*Basic Instinct.*"

"*Basic Instinct*?" I repeated, taking a step back.

"Yeah, why?" Maggie said. "Did you already see it? Don't tell me how it ends!"

"Yes, I've seen it a dozen times," I told her. "It's been on TV for years now."

"Years?" Maggie arched an eyebrow at me. "Ryan, what are you talking about? It came out to the theaters a few weeks ago."

"Noooo," I replied. "It came out in 1992."

"Ryan, this *is* 1992," Maggie insisted.

His Second Chance

"What? What do you mean this is 1992? I'm dreaming that you're here," I uttered, not sure if I believed her. "So far, it's been a great dream. I don't want to wake up."

"No, Ryan, you're not dreaming," Maggie stated. "It's 1992. April 24th, 1992, to be exact."

I stared at her blankly. Words came out of her mouth, but I heard them as if she spoke a language I didn't understand.

"Your 21st birthday is in a few days," she said. "That's why I came to visit you."

What was she saying? My breath left my lungs. My brain stuttered. Every part of me paused while my thoughts caught up. I fell against Prashant's car, as the whole street seemed to swirl around me. I stepped away from Maggie, clutching my head in my hands. Everything resembled what I remembered, yet didn't. The lack of my cell phone. The landline. Prashant dressing like a kid again. Me weighing less. Prashant's old Saab. I was physically in my junior year of college, but I lived through it 25 years earlier. How was that possible? Half-stumbling back, I steadied myself against the side of the car in shock, knocking Maggie's suitcase over. My heart thumped out of my chest. What happened?

I studied my watch again. A gift from my grandparents when I graduated high school, it was a Junghans Mega, the first radio-controlled timepiece ever made. A perfect gift for a computer geek like me. Even though I had to replace the band a few times, the timepiece still ticked. I wiped my eyes and stared at the date display on the face: "FR24. 4.92. 9:53 p.m." I crumpled to a seated position next to the car.

HIS SECOND CHANCE

"Ryan, are you okay?" Maggie pleaded. She stood over me and raised a palm to my sweating forehead. "Are you sick? Do you have a fever? You don't look so good."

"I... I... I thought I dreamt about you," I stuttered. "You're real?"

"Yeah, why wouldn't I be?" Maggie glared at me like I had three heads.

My head spun. I struggled to breathe as air escaped me. "This whole day was so great," I muttered, still trying to find my bearings. "Too good to be in a dream. I would have woken up by now if I was dreaming." I focused on nothing in front of me.

"Ryan, you're scaring me," Maggie's voice fell to a whisper. "What's going on?"

She took my hand warmly in hers and calmness instantly enveloped me. She always had that effect on me, no matter what year it was. Typically, I would never miss an opportunity to put my hand elsewhere but as soon as she held it, my pulse dropped back down into a healthier range. This was what I needed right now.

Somehow, I traveled back in time. How was it possible? I didn't remember anything about yesterday after that street light shattered over my head. Was this related to that explosion in Prashant's lab? Settle down. I needed to think rationally about this. Was this a freak accident or was there some higher purpose as to why this happened to me? Nothing I could do if it's the former. Let's say there's a purpose to it. What purpose? Was this a chance to redo some specific moment or moments in my life? Some items to change jumped into my mind easily—one of the biggest ones stood next to me kissing my forehead with her soft wonderful lips. Maybe it was this.

Maggie squatted next to me.

With my free hand, I trailed a finger along her angelic face and pushed a blonde lock behind her ear. That beautiful face. She was smart and could charm the pants off me. She had the mysterious ability to easily get me to do anything. With Maggie as my arm candy, the envy of my friends boosted my ego. Maggie had everything I wanted and needed, but with her attending Penn across the state, a dedicated relationship was near impossible. We never had an exclusivity talk even though I wasn't going out with anyone else. Maggie was always way out of my league anyway. I never grasped why she chose to date me when she could go out with practically any other guy. What did she see in a geek like me? But here she was, spending her weekend with me for my birthday. Somehow, we made it work but avoided discussing the future.

The future. Yesterday, I was in my mid-40s. Today, I was days away from turning 21. During the 25 years between, Maggie came in and out of my life, but I never stopped loving her, even though I never had the guts to tell her. Wait, was that right? Did I never tell her I loved her? Should I tell her now? No, this was *not* the right moment for a first "I love you". She thought that I was delusional enough.

Mindlessly, I reached for the scar on my right hand, but it was gone. Of course it was, I was in 1992, *before* I met Manju.

HIS SECOND CHANCE

"I'm fine. I swear." I cupped Maggie's face in my hands and kissed her tender lips as a distraction for my new revelation. "I'm sorry I'm being weird. I missed you so much."

"Okay, if you say so," Maggie cooed. "I want you to have a good birthday weekend."

"Now that you are with me, it's already off to a fantastic start." I kissed her again. "Let's go see *Basic Instinct* tomorrow. I hear there's a surprise ending."

We stood and I grabbed Maggie's suitcase again and we sauntered along the sidewalk, hand in hand. We entered my place and headed down the hall to my bedroom to drop her bag off.

When I opened my door, Maggie skirted around me and flopped on my bed. She leaned back on her palms and stared at me with the eyes of a wolf.

"We don't *have* to go to that party yet," she purred.

Oh lord, I was a goner.

I dropped her suitcase on the floor and rushed over to her, kissing her luscious mouth, pushing her backward onto my bed. Straddling her with my legs, I pressed my lower body against her. I tore at her jacket and pulled her T-shirt from her jeans, reaching for her silky skin.

She warmed to my touch. Maggie sucked her stomach in as I trailed my fingers across her belly while I kissed her. We'd be naked soon, but I smiled mischievously into her eyes as I slid my hand down inside of her pants. Ready for my attention, she arched her back towards me and let out a small, soft, sexy moan. God, that moan. I missed that moan.

His Second Chance

I deftly unbuttoned her pants with one hand and quickly pulled them off of her without breaking eye contact. Her panties quickly followed. I was so hungry for her I didn't even take the time to recognize what kind of panties she wore. She gave me a surprised and wanting gaze that urged me to move south. I knew where I would start. On Maggie's sexy right calf were two adorable matching moles sitting next to each other like twins. I missed that leg!

At my first warm kiss, tiny goosebumps developed on her soft skin. I smiled and took my sweet slow time kissing and licking a path up her leg, savoring the sweet taste of her skin. My prize lay up ahead and I fought my urge to jump right into it. As I neared the warm goal that waited for me at the top of her smooth, sexy thigh, the familiarity of a passion I had long forgotten filled my senses. Sights, sounds, and smells urged me to get to the top of my journey and explore.

My lips and tongue took turns exploring her sensitive folds as she wrapped her fingers in my hair and pulled me against her. I softly moaned into her as I reached out with my strong tongue and pressed it slowly up into her sweet tunnel. Her moaning grew louder as she squeezed down on my tongue. I could spend an eternity doing this. But apparently my licks and kisses were too powerful to allow for an indefinite reunion with her fabulous pussy. Maggie's nails dug into my shoulders as my tongue experienced a wonderful sensation.

I unbuttoned her blouse as I kissed a trail up her stomach and between her breasts. I wanted to kiss her soft mouth, but her supple neck distracted me. I missed that neck. It had a way of fitting against my lips perfectly and I could smell her subtle, but intoxicating, perfume. Her neck also put her mouth right next to my ear where she softly cooed, "Oh wow, what do we have down here?"

Her soft, warm hand curled around my cock and somehow made it grow even harder. I smiled at her as I kissed her face and caressed her hair. She was as hot as I ever remembered. "How badly do you want to be inside me?" she asked. Oh, I was a goner.

"I'd kill or die," I answered. This wasn't the first time I had said this. That phrase had become a catch-phrase in our time together ... and I meant every word of it. I grabbed a condom out of my dresser drawer and, for the next hour, I made good on my intention. Our natural bodies never separated; I almost forgot how sexy it was that Maggie preferred to be on top.

When we finally came up for air, "Wow," Maggie puffed into my ear. "You missed me, huh?"

"You have no idea," I said, kissing her lips. "Like I haven't seen you in forever."

"I won't need to go to the gym for a few days," she chuckled, trailing her finger along my bare chest.

"You're amazing," I told her. "I love being with you."

I held her next to me. Nestled comfortably in my arms on my bed, her naked body warmed against mine. The line blurred where my body ended and hers began.

After we laid in bed a little while longer, we dressed for the fraternity party and headed out the door.

HIS SECOND CHANCE

Chapter 5

Ten minutes later, Maggie and I sauntered up to the front door of the Alpha Tau Omega house. On the Greek Quad, the plain, red-brick, three-story building gave the appearance of a 1970s apartment building rather than a fraternity house. Greek letters of ATΩ on the side of the building proclaimed otherwise.

I knocked on the door at the first-floor main entrance. Rock music blared from the inside.

Being roommates with Prashant had its privileges: he belonged to the ATΩ fraternity—but didn't fit the stereotype. Almost all of his brothers were on the football team and spent most of their time on the gridiron or at the gym. Prashant was recruited as a sophomore because the president of the fraternity discovered that he was an exceptional engineer and begged him to be the top mechanic for the house buggy.

Buggy racing was a blue-chip obsession at Carnegie Mellon since the 1920s. With a university full of engineers, physicists, and mathletes like Prashant and me, race day at Spring Carnival was like the Olympics. Every April, students lined the streets of nearby Schenley Park cheering on stealth-like small aerodynamic vehicles, powered only by gravity and human pushers. Like an ice hockey goalie, the solo driver had to be a special kind of crazy to race down hills face-first at 30 miles an hour. Since it was already late April, I assumed the races took place a couple of weeks earlier.

Like a pit crew at a NASCAR race, Prashant was the top mechanic to repair his fraternity's buggy if it ever crashed. His brothers relied on him to keep the buggy in top shape. Since Prashant spent a lot of time at the fraternity house, his friends welcomed me in the process. Prashant hadn't introduced me to all of the brothers yet, but the ones I met were civilized.

"Hey, Ryan," a towering frat brother assigned as the gatekeeper to the party said to me as Maggie and I stood before him. His job for the night was to allow as many girls in as possible and keep the guys limited to the guest list. The ratio of guys to girls on campus was eight to one so girls were allowed practically anywhere. Sometimes I struggled to get into other parties, but being Prashant's roommate gave me lifetime access to his fraternity house.

The gatekeeper eyed up Maggie with a wicked smile. Of course he did—she was hot. He stood a good five inches taller than me and had 75 pounds on me. I bet he played linebacker.

"Hi, Mike," I said, grabbing Maggie's hand. "Have you met Maggie?"

"No," Mike replied, easing up his once-over on my date. "Good to meet you. Come on in."

"Thanks," Maggie said. "Is Prashant here?"

His Second Chance

"Yeah, he's inside somewhere," Mike answered. "Last I saw him, he headed to the green room."

"Geez," I chuckled, realizing what he meant.

Maggie and I maneuvered our way around Mike and entered a hallway filled with a bunch of partygoers with cups of beer in their hands. Several of the guys nodded to me in acknowledgment in the middle of their conversations. Music from Pearl Jam blasted through the large house speakers that hung high on the walls.

Holding Maggie's hand, I led her through the labyrinth of people in the hallway and into the main party room. A few dozen people filled the space, downing beers, dancing, and playing beer pong on the far side of the room. A lot of Prashant's fraternity brothers proudly wore ATΩ T-shirts, exposing their bulky biceps. Maybe this was their way of silently intimidating their guests since most of the football players couldn't compete in the classrooms?

"Want a beer?" I asked Maggie.

"Yeah, sure."

She followed me to the keg in the corner of the room. I grabbed two plastic cups from a nearby table and filled them for us.

"Come on," I said, "let's go find Prashant."

We wound our way out of the main party room and back into the hall, heading toward the back end of the building. We entered the next room and stumbled back into the hallway from the stench. The Green Room earned its moniker from everyone smoking weed in it. A dusty cloud filled the room, giving it an angelic form.

Maggie rubbed her eyes from the thick haze.

"I swear I'll get high from standing here," she gulped.

His Second Chance

"Yeah," I agreed, downing my beer.

I visually searched the room and found Prashant through the billowing fog, heading toward us.

"Hey, Maggie!" Prashant stepped up to us and gave her a hug. "Good to see you again. Didn't think I'd see you until tomorrow."

"You, too," she replied. "How've you been?"

"Prashant, what're you doing in here?" I asked, interrupting Prashant.

"Relax, *Dad*, I'm not smoking," he countered, presenting empty hands to us. "I was talking to Kai over there. He's a Freshman. He's helping me with buggy next year and then take over after I graduate." Prashant nodded to one of the few non-football players in the house standing near a couch which had seen better days. Kai stood 5'6" at best and appeared thinner than me. Perfect for a buggy mechanic.

Maggie rubbed her eyes again, silently pleading with me to help her escape the drug-induced fog.

"Let's get outta here," I told them.

Prashant led us out of The Green Room and back into the large party room.

As we entered the space, several of Prashant's fraternity brothers slapped him on the shoulder in a good-natured way, almost knocking him to the floor with their sheer strength. I recognized most of them from previous parties but didn't remember all of their names. Each one of them towered over Prashant and could easily crush him.

His Second Chance

We made our way to the keg again and I filled my cup again. I chugged it immediately.

Prashant led Maggie and me through the crowd to one of his brothers. He motioned to us and then back to the brother who stood before him. "Jim, this is Ryan and Maggie. Ryan's my roommate."

"Oh yeah," Jim bellowed. "I've heard about you." He faced Maggie and half-bent down in front of her. In an instant, he circled her tiny waist with his tree-trunk arms and lifted her right off the floor. She didn't stand a fighting chance to object.

Maggie squealed in delight as Jim lifted her high above everyone's heads, a view she rarely had. She braced herself against his chest to prevent herself from tumbling to the ground. He already had several beers and wasn't as coordinated as she hoped. As quickly as Jim lifted Maggie, he gently put her back down on the floor.

"You're small enough to be a buggy driver," Jim told her. "We should recruit you."

Maggie blushed.

"Size doesn't matter when you're horizontal." I flexed my beer muscles.

Maggie glared at me with daggers for eyes, slicing through my soul. She purposefully took a step away from me. Her hands formed into tiny fists. Maggie's cheeks turned a deep crimson. A low growl emitted from her throat. I thought I was adding to the playful atmosphere with my drunken, stupid comment, but apparently Maggie didn't think so.

His Second Chance

"Aww, man, what's the matter with you?" a voice behind me bellowed. "Why would you say that about her?"

I turned around and came face to face with a chest of ATΩ letters. The owner of the body glared down at me, a warm smile formed on his face.

He shouldered past me like a giant parting trees in his way and approached Maggie.

"Hi, I'm Mav-- I mean Brett." He closed the space between them and offered his hand to her.

"Which is it? Mav or Brett?" she asked, accepting his gentlemanly gesture.

Brett chuckled at Maggie's confusion. "It's Brett, but the guys call me Maverick."

"I'm Maggie," she replied, focusing all of her attention on him. Her mouth curved upward and I could tell immediately that she found Brett hot. What girl wouldn't? He kept his brown, wavy hair trimmed short and could have passed for a young and tall Tom Cruise. His deep cheek dimple and model good looks undoubtedly won over all the girls. Brett was toned but didn't appear gargantuan like some of the other football players around us. He probably had an eight pack under that fraternity T-shirt. I hated him.

"Maggie?" I called after her, to no answer. So much for reveling in seeing other guys hit on her. I was an idiot. My premonition got the best of me.

Chapter 6

"Dude, you're book-smart, but you're dumber than a box of rocks," Prashant scolded me.

"Wha-at?" I shot back.

"Maggie," he stated. "Even though you don't think you were out of line, if you don't go apologize to her, she'll stay here with Maverick and you'll have a date with Rosie Palm and her five friends later tonight."

"Ugh, you're right," I lamented. "I hate it when you're right. I screwed up." I had spent the last hour stewing over Maggie and Brett talking in the corner. I thought I was smarter than that. Hadn't my maturity increased with my age?

I stared as Maggie laughed at Brett's dumb jokes and stood within inches of him. Occasionally, she glared over at me, making sure I watched. Which I was. How would I fix this? I had hoped the time-traveling made things better, not worse. Wasn't that why I was given a second chance to do things over?

Prashant followed my gaze. "Now would be good."

His Second Chance

I huffed at him and stepped over to Maggie and Brett. She didn't stop talking to him to acknowledge me. I deserved that.

"Maggie," I whispered, glancing to one side and then the other. Why did I sense like I interrupted them?

She didn't respond.

"Maggie," I spoke a little louder.

Still no response.

"Maggie!"

Annoyed, she finally took notice of me. "What do you want, Ryan? I'm busy with Brett." She crossed her arms against her chest in a snit.

"I'd like to talk to you," I said. "Please."

"Fine," she replied. She turned to Brett. "I'm so sorry. I'll be right back."

Maggie turned to me and huffed as she shouldered past me. I stood there a moment gaping at her. She stopped two steps later and turned back to face me. "Let's go. You wanted to talk."

Then I followed her into the hallway. Even though she was clearly pissed at me, I couldn't keep my eyes off of her ass as she strutted ahead of me.

Maggie found a quiet section in the hall and finally held my attention.

"Well?" She pushed both fists into her tiny hips.

Her exasperation threw me. We usually got along without discontent so I wasn't sure how to calm her down. The unfamiliar waters baffled me.

"I'm—I'm sorry," I told her.

His Second Chance

"What the hell's the matter with you?" she shot back, slicing through my bullshit answer. Even though she stood several inches shorter than me, she stared me down, unblinking. Her take-no-prisoners attitude made me want her even more.

"Um—I—" My mind went blank. She usually didn't overreact like this so I wasn't sure how to respond.

"Forget it!" Maggie attempted to push past me again, but I snagged her arm before she could go any further, back to Brett.

"Maggie, wait, please," I pleaded, releasing her arm. "I'm sorry for what I said. I was out of line."

"You embarrassed me!" she shrieked, pointing a finger at me. "You're such a jerk."

"I know. I'm sorry." I lowered my eyes in shame. She was right. My insecurity reared its ugly head and I wanted to act macho in front of the massive football players, but mortified her in the process. I really didn't think what I said was that mortifying, but she apparently did. Downing two cups of beer in ten minutes hadn't helped either. I glanced through the doorway of the party room at Brett chatting with Prashant. I hoped they weren't making fun of what an idiot I was. I didn't mean to be.

I spoke again, "If you want to hang out with Brett—"

"What? Do you think you could stop me?" Maggie countered, boasting her independence. One of the things I loved about her. She followed my gaze and peered at Brett a moment. "He's a nice guy, but—"

"But what?" I begged the question.

She blew out a sigh.

His Second Chance

"But he's not you, you big jerk." Maggie punched me in the arm. "Don't ever embarrass me like that again, okay?"

"Never again." I raised my right hand to her. God, I was such a douche. I was convinced I traveled back in time to make things better, not worse. "I swear."

My heart warmed that Maggie chose me over Brett. I never considered myself a pocket-protector nerd like a lot of the awkward guys on campus who clammed up when a girl spoke to them, but being around muscle-filled football players who got by on their looks made my insecurity rear its ugly head. Maggie didn't deserve that. Maggie was the first girl who I pursued. In high school I only dated because those girls pursued me. I could never muster the courage to go after a hot girl that I wanted to date. As I aged, my confidence around women surged. Maggie was the reason for that.

She took a step closer to me and finally smiled at me. I hated that Maggie was agitated with me and promised myself that I would never let it happen again if I could. Now that I failed my first test of doing things over, I hoped to turn every future event for the better. I took Maggie's hand in mine, leaned in, and kissed her on the cheek. "You're amazing, you know that."

She flashed me a secret gaze that made me believe I stood a foot taller. She always made me feel like she was 100% there for me. No lip service.

"I know." She chuckled.

Chapter 7

The next morning, Maggie and I sat at my kitchen table eating the eggs and toast I made us. She looked adorable in my T-shirt and silky maroon boxers. Her blonde hair was pulled into a topknot on her head and she wore glasses. If a girl could be cute and sexy at the same time, she nailed it. She flipped through my hard copy of *The Pelican Brief* while munching on the remains of her toast. I sat at the table with her, staring at her beautiful face. My half-eaten plate of eggs and a can of Jolt cola rested on the table in front of me.

My behavior at the party the night before still humbled me, but I didn't want to sound like a sap and continually apologize for it. Fortunately, Maggie forgave me and the make-up sex last night was incredible. But I never wanted to be put in that situation again where I might lose her.

"Maggie," I blurted, "you know I like you, right?"

"What? Yeah, of course," she mumbled, still mesmerized by the pages. "I like you, too."

His Second Chance

"No, I mean I *really* like you," I told her. I took a long swig of Jolt, unorthodox for breakfast, biding time for her to reply.

She still didn't turn her face up, despite my best efforts to get her attention. Admittedly, I was never one to profess my feelings to her so she thought light of the conversation. We avoided an exclusivity talk before, but I needed to rectify my mistake. In college, I didn't date anyone else and I was pretty sure she didn't, even though I never asked her. We always made plans to see each other every month or so. Were we dating but without talking about?

"Maggie, I'm trying to tell you something." I slipped my hand under the front cover of the book and, in one motion, snapped it shut. Startled, she jumped back in response.

"Okay! Sorry! I'm listening." She finally found my eyes with hers. "What do you want to tell me?"

"I'm trying to tell you that I like you," I repeated.

"Yeah, I like you too, Ryan. Why else do you think I would travel across the state to visit you?" Her mouth curved upward into a sweet, toothy grin. God, she was so cute.

"And I'm happy you did." I took her hand in mine. "But what will we do when you go back to school?"

"Talk on the phone like we always do," she answered.

"No, I mean after that," I sighed. "Like when I graduate next year—and then when you graduate the following year."

"Oh," Maggie uttered, slipping her hand from mine. "I hadn't thought of that. Well, I don't expect you to wait for me. That wouldn't be fair. Don't get me wrong, I like you and all, but we have to be realistic."

His Second Chance

"But what if I want to?" I told her. "I like being with you and I don't mind waiting for you to graduate. We've been able to meet up with each other pretty often, even being across the state, so I don't see how we can't continue to do that."

"Wouldn't it depend where you get a job?" Maggie countered. "And then where I get a job?" Maggie studied Art History at Penn. "I want to go to a big museum if I can, and that might not be in Pennsylvania."

"We can make it work," I reassured her. I already knew my first job out of college was with Deloitte assigned in Florida. It was further away, but I knew I'd have enough money to fly back and forth to see her a couple of times a month.

"But what if I'm in, say, Boston, and you're in LA?" she questioned. She took my hand in hers again. "I like you and I adore your enthusiasm, but we have to be practical." I admired her logic, but I couldn't tell her that we could make it work because I didn't want to tell her about how I traveled in time. The answers still eluded me. If I had to repeat my entire senior year of college to be with Maggie, I would do it. I wasn't sure how the time travel affected me yet, but I knew I wanted to make things different with Maggie. She was worth it.

I blew out a heavy sigh and gulped down the rest of the Jolt cola. I needed to convince her to date me after graduation. If I didn't, then we'd end up at the same original crossroads and we might go our separate paths again. The first time around I didn't tell her that I wanted to date her and I lost her. I won't make the same mistake again. I missed my chance the first time to have happiness with Maggie and I kicked myself for years. That can't happen again.

"I wish I could be more in your life, but I love that you don't need me," I told her. "I love that you're independent. I love that you tell me things because you want to."

"Well, I don't need anyone, but I want to be with you," Maggie replied. "Even if it's for the next year. We can figure out the future later. We have time."

Convincing Maggie would be harder than I thought.

* * * *

Later that night, Maggie and I exited the movie theater hand in hand. We spent the entire time watching *Basic Instinct* with her head on my shoulder. Even though our conversation about the future that morning didn't draw a conclusion, I still wanted to enjoy every minute I could spend with Maggie. I walked on the outside of the sidewalk, to protect her even if she didn't need it.

"I can't believe that ending," she gasped.

"I told you," I chuckled.

We left Manor Theater in Squirrel Hill, a good mile from Beeler Street. Strolling down Murray Avenue, we passed a closed-for-the-night bagel shop and a florist. A few other people wandered down the sidewalk under the guidance of the streetlights; one fizzled out above us. The half-moon in the dark sky set the romantic scene. Silence comforted me like I had never experienced before.

His Second Chance

As we approached the intersection of Murray and Wilkins Avenue, I stopped. The commercial buildings had eased into red brick houses that shared a narrow yard between them.

"Is something wrong?" Maggie asked me.

"No," I said. "I wanted to do this."

I cupped her chin in my hand and moved my face closer to hers. I kissed her tender lips and a slight moan escaped from her mouth. The natural reactions she gave me ushered me to another place. I didn't care if anyone on the street witnessed us making out.

"Stay with me," I whispered in her ear.

"What?" Maggie chuckled through a smile.

"Stay here, in Pittsburgh, with me," I repeated, moving her to face me. "I hate being without you."

"Ryan, I can't," Maggie responded. "I have class Monday morning."

Unbeknownst to her, Maggie was right. She had to finish college before she could be with me. She had to get on the train the next morning and head back to Philly. My soul died every time we parted. She could talk about the shape of a tree and I wouldn't care. Maggie mesmerized me more than she could fathom and made things better for me. I never wanted to be without her again. My heart stopped every time we were together.

Fifteen minutes later, I opened the door to my bedroom for us.

Standing in my room, I took Maggie's chin in my fingertips and kissed her lips as gently as I could. Those amazing lips. A warm moan escaped from her mouth.

HIS SECOND CHANCE

Maggie stood still as I ran my finger along her collarbone and traced the edge of her white T-shirt. I reached lower to her waist and pulled her top out of her jeans and lifted it over her head. Maggie attempted to grab at my shirt, but I stopped her by grasping her wrist.

"No," I whispered. "Tonight is all about you." I led her to the edge of my bed. "Allow me."

Maggie smiled as I knelt before her, unbuttoned her jeans, slid them down her legs, and removed them. She stood before me in her bra and panties. So sexy. She was the most beautiful woman I had ever met. Her curves could set the bar for ski moguls. I loved staring at her. She was everything to me. I realized I was sent back to have a second chance with Maggie.

I laid Maggie back on my bed, kissing her stomach. Her skin fluttered under my touch, giving me the vindication that I made her feel so good. I inched my way to the top of her panties and traced my finger along the inside of the waistband.

"You're torturing me," Maggie puffed out.

I smiled in pride and continued my prowl down to her sweet pussy. Hooking a finger into her panties, I leisurely pulled them down her silken legs. I planted tiny kisses on her ankle and worked my way back up to her luscious thigh. With my hands under her bare ass, I leaned in and licked her amazing pussy. Maggie arched her body as I darted my tongue in and out of her.

Oh, the pleasure. I could barely focus. Maggie charged my neurons as I tasted her honeyed pussy. I loved making her vulnerable and that she let me take over her body. I licked at her until her body

His Second Chance

writhed in front of me. Experiencing a pussy like hers was the definition of my sexuality.

"Please don't stop," Maggie begged. "I'm so close."

Her wish was my command. I dipped my tongue deeper inside her and found a rhythm that she loved. Soon enough, Maggie moaned as her juices flowed into my mouth. I lapped at her as fast as I could to catch her overflow. Her body shuffled under me and I edged my way up her. I kissed her soft mouth.

"Give me your hand," Maggie whispered. She took my hand in hers and placed it on her racing heart. "You did this to me." My heart beated as fast as hers.

"I've missed you so much, baby," I said to her as my forehead rested on hers and our hearts pounded against each other. We went from a figurative dreamland to a literal one within minutes. Something about having her in my arms was like a sedative. I was relaxed and bathed in feelings of love and satisfaction.

Oh my god, I thought to myself for the one-millionth time that evening. She owned me. The power she held over me was enigmatic. Nothing could keep me from focusing on how wonderful it was to be together and so tightly joined in the throes of passion we shared. I was hers and she was mine.

Maggie relaxed beneath me. I could still touch her lightly clenching my hand as our bodies relaxed into each other and sleep toxins invaded my bloodstream. As much as I wanted to stay awake and love on her until dawn, my body had a different idea.

After our heart rates returned to a healthy pace, I pulled off my clothes and we quickly passed out together. I was in heaven with her

His Second Chance

warm cheeks using my chest for a pillow and her hair on my face with that familiar scent I had missed so much.

At some point during the night, Maggie had donned my favorite college sweatshirt and nothing else. It was long enough to cover her cute bottom—but not by much. She was the epitome of sexy.

I held her in my arms as we spooned.

"This sweatshirt smells like you," she sighed.

Her head nestled back against my neck. Sleep overtook me after our interlude and, with my arms wrapped tightly around her, I laid on a cloud and everything was perfect.

I dropped into a deep sleep with a smile on my face and my love in my arms.

HIS SECOND CHANCE

Chapter 8

The next morning, I awoke from my dream but didn't open my eyes yet. I wanted to enjoy that in-between feeling of being drunk off my dream and not missing a moment with Maggie before she left for Penn.

I blindly reached for her, expecting to graze her soft skin under my touch. But my hand grasped pockets of air instead.

Alarmed, my eyes shot open. Where was she?

Instead of finding Maggie naked in my bed, my neck ached from my head being propped against a red brick wall. My body slumped into a cinder block alcove and I sat on a weathered cement bench. The red brick wall extended beyond me. Four-story buildings in the same crimson brick stretched above the wall.

Several people strolled in front of me. Birds chirped in overhead trees. Two women sat on a nearby bench like mine examining a map. A mom squatted down in front of a baby stroller and offered ice cream to her wispy-haired toddler.

Where was I?

His Second Chance

It could have been Pittsburgh, but nothing specific around me told me I was still there.

Taking a deep breath, I stood from my cement, napping corner. The grey and red brick plaza beneath my feet had smoothed over the years. Several towering trees lined the wide pathway of the plaza. A tall statue of a man on a horse guarded the entrance twenty yards away. Maybe the front of the statue could give me a clue as to where I was.

I hustled the sixty feet to the statue and gazed up to the front of the monument.

The engraved letters on the front provided me the answer: PAUL REVERE.

How the hell did I get to Boston?

The last thing I remembered was being in Maggie's arms. Where was she? And why was I in Boston?

I studied the watch on my right wrist. "SA10. 6.95. 1:17 p.m."

June 10, 1995? How did I skip three years? Obviously, I traveled in time again—but how? And why? Somebody or something was fucking with me and I didn't like it. A cool breeze pricked my body, making me wish I had a sweatshirt.

As I stumbled past the statue of Paul Revere, a large church came into sight across the street. Out of habit, I tapped the back pocket of my pants to confirm if my wallet was still there. A small bulge filled the space. Hopefully, I had some cash in there to pay for any provisions I might need, otherwise I could pillage the collection basket at the church.

His Second Chance

I pulled my wallet out and fanned through a few twenties. Good. Until I could figure out how to use a future credit card, cash could get me by. Good thing it was common knowledge that the commuter trains around the city were cheap. I needed to hoard my cash.

I hooked a left out of Paul Revere Mall onto the sidewalk. The street sign above me said Hanover Street. I made my way past several restaurants, a dry cleaners, another church, and a wine and spirit shop. A double-wide line of red bricks on the sidewalk designating the Freedom Trail veered off to the left as I approached a long line of customers waiting to get into Mike's Pastry. The delicious cannoli inside the single-story brown and red building could wait. I wasn't sure where I was headed, but maybe walking a few blocks could give me some clarity.

A mass of people filled the narrow sidewalks of the North End trying to get in and out of the restaurants and shops. Large banners strapped to the second stories flapped in the wind, touting the name of each restaurant. Sweet aromas of garlic, onion, and freshly baked bread filled the air. Delivery trucks and taxis rumbled down the street next to me.

Ahead of me, kids bundled in colorful sweatshirts played in the lush grass of the Rose Kennedy Greenway.

As I approached Congress Street, rainbow-colored banners and flags filled City Hall Plaza. Hundreds of people waved miniature rainbow flags on both sides of the street. Music from Queen blared from overhead speakers. Pride Fest.

His Second Chance

My friend Russell and his boyfriend took me to Pride Fest in Pittsburgh when we were in undergrad by convincing me that I would meet bisexual girls. Heterosexuals like myself didn't usually publicly mix with gays at CMU because nobody took them seriously. Even though I was initially reluctant, Russell and his boyfriend introduced me to a lot of terrific people and festivities. Russell now lived in Orlando, but wouldn't it be funny if I encountered him at this Pride Fest?

I ambled past groups of people holding brightly colored signs proclaiming, "Love is Love." Most of the straight and gay onlookers observed a small parade featuring different LGBTQ groups. The uplifting music and atmosphere were inspiring. As much as I wanted to stay and absorb the festivities, something inside me told me to keep going.

In the compact plaza, near the stairs on the left side of City Hall, a group of artists sitting in folding chairs with matching easels caught my attention. A lot of the artists happily painted animal faces on laughing children. From the backside, I stopped and witnessed the exchange between one of the female artists and a young girl with golden curly hair. The young woman painted a pink tiger on the little girl's face.

"There," the young woman said, putting the finishing touches on her masterpiece. "You look beautiful."

The little girl beamed with pride. "Thank you!" she gushed.

"Get out there and let them hear you roar!" the woman told her. The little girl gave her best roar. With that, the woman turned in my direction and I recognized her immediately.

His Second Chance

"Maggie?" I called to her. She wore paint-stained overalls, a tie-dyed long-sleeved shirt, and Birkenstocks. Her blonde hair cascaded down her back. She oozed cuteness.

She focused on the path where her name was being called and locked eyes with me.

"Ryan?" Maggie's face glowed like a ray of sunshine. That face. She was the reason why I came to Boston and jumped ahead three years. I knew it.

I ran over to her, bustling past a few onlookers who gave me an annoyed grimace when I knocked into them. She stood from her chair and gazed at me.

"You look great!" I swallowed her up in my arms.

I cupped her face with my hands and attempted to kiss her lips, but she backed off to stop me.

Noticing her hesitancy, I halted. "I'm sorry," I said. "I'm so happy to see you."

"It's okay," she said. "What are you doing here? Do you live in Boston?"

"No, I—I—I'm in town for a few days," I kind of lied to her. I wasn't sure how long I would be in Boston, but I knew I didn't live there. Hell, I didn't even have a change of clothes.

"I can't believe you found me in all these people." She raised her arm in a sweeping motion toward the crowd around us. "How long's it been? Five years?"

"No," I corrected her. I couldn't tell her I saw her yesterday, but if I calculated correctly, less time had passed. "Three years."

His Second Chance

"Three years?" Maggie arched an eyebrow at me. "No, that can't be right. I was in Paris three years ago. Studying at all of the art museums. I was there all of my sophomore year. My professors always told me that I was one of the youngest students in the program."

Huh? How did I not know that? Maggie never told me she was heading to Paris when we first started dating her freshman year. What did I miss? Did something happen in my last time jump? Did I miss an entire chunk of her life? But she couldn't understand that I traveled back in time. I still wasn't sure how or why it happened, but it would freak her out if I told her what was happening to me. I had to pretend that I was in 1995 with her and didn't have knowledge of an alternate time path.

"Oh, right," I fibbed. "I must have gotten my dates mixed up." I studied her for a moment. "When was the last time we saw each other?" I wanted her to tell me so that I could collaborate on her answer.

"I think it was the end of your sophomore year and I was a freshman," she said. "You never gave me a reason to be exclusive with you so I let things go and didn't pursue you. That's when I decided to go to Paris."

Good grief, I was such a dipshit. How could I be so stupid to never tell her I wanted to date her exclusively? Somehow, I screwed up again. I had to rectify it. She was the most wonderful girl I had ever met. Dating her while she went to Penn and I was at Carnegie Mellon was difficult because of the distance, but I never considered that we *wouldn't* be together.

His Second Chance

But finding her in Boston was kismet. Our paths had crossed again and it had to mean something. It had to. Why else was I there? I was given another opportunity to make things right again.

"Oh, right. I'm so sorry," I told her, giving her a once-over. "But you look great. You really do."

She chuckled like I didn't get a joke.

"Do you have plans tonight?" she asked me.

I loved her bold attitude. My mind wandered to the first time we had sex and she left me a note saying next time she wanted to be on top. Her boldness was intoxicating.

"No," I replied. "What are you thinking?"

She motioned to her painting easel. "I'm almost done here, so if you give me a few minutes, I'd love to have dinner with you tonight. We can hang at my place this afternoon. I'm pretty sure I have a bottle of red at home."

"Yes!" I gushed. "I'd love to." I couldn't wait to peel off her overalls and discover what I could find underneath.

Fifteen minutes later, I followed Maggie through the Pride Fest crowd heading south on Congress Street. We found our way to Haymarket Station and hopped the Orange Line. With her art supplies, Maggie stood a good foot away from me on the subway. Close enough that she was in my company but not near enough for my taste. I wanted to run my hand up and down her ass and didn't care if anyone else on the train witnessed me do it.

We departed the subway at the Back Bay Station. Maggie led me down Dartmouth Street as she lugged her painting supplies in a five-gallon bucket.

HIS SECOND CHANCE

"Let me carry that for you," I offered.

"Nah, I'm fine," she replied, holding her bucket in her left hand. "I'm used to it."

Even though Maggie wouldn't let me help her, I scurried around to her right side and walked between her and the edge of the sidewalk.

Along Dartmouth, we passed a few small restaurants and bars. Cars whizzed by us on the road. Flower pots hung from second and third story window sills. We headed to a more residential area of downtown.

I casually grabbed for Maggie's free hand, grazing her fingers with mine.

"Ummm ... What are you doing?" she questioned, pulling her hand away from mine.

Quickly realizing I was out of line, I purposely took a step away from her, playing it off. "Oh, sorry ... I ... didn't mean to," I stuttered, taken aback that she rejected me.

Obviously, Maggie hadn't remembered how we used to hold hands while walking down the street when we dated. What other changes in her life had my time-traveling affected?

A half-block later, we stopped on the sidewalk.

"This is my place," Maggie stated as we stood in front of a red brick walkup with a black double-door. Matching rowhomes lined the street. If someone was drunk, they might stumble into the wrong one, because they all conformed. I followed her up the stairs. Her hips swayed in perfect rhythm as she ascended the grey cement steps. Even though she didn't want me holding her hand, I could still admire her fine ass.

Maggie keyed us in and we climbed wooden stairs to the third floor. Maggie unlocked another door marked with "3B" on the front.

"Welcome to my humble abode," Maggie said as she ushered me into her small apartment. She dropped the bucket of art supplies on the floor once I stepped inside. She led me to a small living room where a couch kept company with a large drawing easel and tubes of different colors of paint. A peace lily filled a colorful pot on the floor in the corner. The kitchen bent off to the left where a small table and two chairs patiently waited for diners. I assumed a bedroom was down the opposite hallway.

"It's cute," I told her.

"It's tiny, but I don't care," she said. "I can take the T to work and walk to practically anything I need."

"Where are you working?" I begged the question.

"The Museum of Fine Arts," she replied. "In the Stars of Paris Exhibition. I love it."

"That's a huge step from painting animal faces on kids," I joked with her.

"Yeah, but that gets me working with the little ones," she said. "Believe it or not, not many kids are interested in Henri de Toulouse-Lautrec." Maggie chuckled at her own joke.

"No! Really!"

We both laughed.

His Second Chance

I remembered how Maggie loved little kids. If she saw kids near us, she always knelt down to their level, chatted with them, and made them feel important. They adored her. She was like the Pied Piper and they followed her around. One day, she would be a great mom.

"But seriously, that's a great job. I always knew you were destined for success," I told her. "I knew it the first time I met you."

Maggie blushed and turned her face away from me for a moment.

She broke the silence by asking, "Where are you staying tonight?" She motioned to her compact room. "You can stay here if you want."

"Seriously? Are you sure? I don't want to impose." I didn't understand her mixed signals, but I wouldn't complain.

"I insist," Maggie replied. "Why would you not stay here? We've known each other for a long time. I still can't believe you found me today."

Visions of kissing Maggie entered my mind. Even though she didn't remember us holding hands, she might remember more when I kissed her. I wanted to climb into her bed and pleasure her the whole night. All I needed was some liquid courage.

Interrupting my fantasy, Maggie ventured into her minuscule kitchen and I trailed behind her. Like the few furnishings in the family room, it housed a fridge, a stove, a sink, and not much else. In the corner of the countertop next to a half-used loaf of bread, Maggie eyed a small vase of purple tulips. She smiled wide, took two strides, and opened the accompanying little white envelope.

His Second Chance

She beamed as she read the card. I couldn't help but wonder who they were from. Her birthday was a month earlier, so what was the occasion? Whoever sent them remembered that tulips were her favorite.

"They're from TJ," she gushed as she read the card out loud. *"Sorry I missed you this morning. Can't wait to see you!"*

TJ? Who the hell was TJ?

Chapter 9

A knock at the front door shelved my jealous thoughts.

Maggie pushed past me and headed to her door. She opened it to a tall, curvy brunette holding several take-out containers in her hands. The woman wore faded jeans and a white tank top. The edge of a black, lacy bra peeked out from the side of the tank top.

"I barely had time to change at home and get us food. They didn't have the shrimp spring rolls that you wanted," the woman rattled off to Maggie, "so I got you veggie instead."

"That's fine, I don't care," Maggie responded. "Thanks!"

Maggie followed the woman chatting into the kitchen as I trailed behind like a kid following his parents through a bookstore. Obviously, the woman knew her way around Maggie's apartment. She plopped the takeout containers on the countertop as Maggie opened the fridge to get some drinks.

"Who's this?" the woman finally acknowledged me.

"I'm Ryan," I told her, pointing to myself.

His Second Chance

"We've been friends for a long time," Maggie interrupted from the fridge. "When I first started Penn."

"Oh, right. I'm Tamara." Maggie's friend offered her hand to me. "Funny ... Maggie and I met at Penn senior year."

I shook Tamara's hand and she smirked at me like I missed a joke again.

"I hope you like Chinese," she told me. "Eat dinner with us. And then we'll all go out for drinks when we're done so that I can get to know you better."

Was this woman hitting on me? Since Maggie was dating some guy named TJ, I would adjust my crush for the night. Tamara was a smoky alternative, even though I preferred blondes.

Maggie strode over to us. "Sorry, no red wine, but I have beer instead." She handed me an opened bottle of Sam Adams. A puff of pressurized steam wisped into the air. She gave a similar bottle to Tamara and kept one for herself.

She raised her bottle in a toast; Tamara and I followed suit. "To old friends," Maggie stated.

"To old friends," Tamara and I echoed.

We all clinked the glass bottles and downed half of our beers.

Maggie grabbed a few plates and utensils from the cabinets and set them on her kitchen table. Tamara turned back to the take-out food and opened the bags, putting three small white cardboard boxes and two wax paper bags on the counter.

"We have General Tso's, Lo Mein, fried rice, and veggie spring rolls," she announced. "Ryan, I hope you like them."

His Second Chance

"It's all good," I answered. I liked Tamara's boldness and take-charge attitude. No wonder Maggie liked her. Any friend of Maggie's was a friend of mine. This could turn into a great night. We could all go dancing, sing karaoke, and stay out until all hours doing shots. I would take full advantage of being out on the town with two hot women.

Tamara turned back and faced Maggie. "Those flowers look great, don't they?"

"Yes, they do," Maggie answered. She took a step closing the gap between her and Tamara. "Thank you so much for them. I love them."

Maggie slipped an arm around Tamara's waist, pulled her closer, and planted a kiss on Tamara's lips. "Just like I love you."

The scene in front of me sent my mind reeling and my mouth fell open. I couldn't comprehend the image without uttering nonsense. "What? ... How? ... Who? ... I ... You ... We ..."

"Ryan, are you okay?" Maggie broke her embrace with Tamara and eyed me suspiciously.

"I ... I ..." I uttered. My feet cemented to the floor and my arms refused to move. My heart thumped inside my chest like a woodpecker begging to get out. Several bullets of sweat sprung up on my forehead.

"Have you never seen two women kiss before?" Tamara joked. She kissed Maggie again. "We're allowed, y'know."

Finally finding function in my body, I chugged what was left of my beer. Then I grabbed Maggie's bottle out of her free hand and downed her beer as well.

His Second Chance

"Ryan!" Maggie squawked. "Seriously, are you okay? What's the matter with you?"

Maggie and Tamara were a couple? How did this happen? What did I miss? Oh my god, I made Maggie hate men! I never told her I loved her and she went the opposite way. The far, far opposite way. I fucked up. How could we ever get back together now that she was a lesbian? What did I do to change the course of our lives? She and I were meant to be together, not her and Tamara. But how long would I be in Boston? How long would I be tortured watching Maggie make out with another girl? I had to find answers. And fast.

Gulping down a huge breath, I finally settled down into the nearest chair. My heart rate was almost back to its normal pace.

"I'm okay, I swear," I half-lied, wiping the newly formed sweat from my brow.

I glanced over at the vase of daisies, narrowing my eyes. "You said the flowers were from TJ."

"They are," Maggie replied, pointing to her girlfriend and wrapping an arm around her waist. "TJ. Tamara Jo."

HIS SECOND CHANCE

Chapter 10

After Maggie, Tamara, and I finished our Chinese, we cleared the dishes, headed out the door, and down the interior steps of Maggie's apartment building. I didn't know if I would get used to Maggie flirting with Tamara, but I had to keep cool otherwise I might raise jealous suspicions with them. I wanted to avoid that at all costs.

Once we stepped outside, Maggie glanced at her watch. "It's after six. Let's go down to Queen Bee for some drinks."

"Good idea," Tamara replied. "Let's show Ryan our city."

"It's a five-minute walk," Maggie explained to me. "Right around the corner."

We hooked a right out of Maggie's walk-up onto Dartmouth Street. At the next intersection, the girls turned right again onto Warren Avenue and I kept pace with them. We passed more red brick walk-ups on one side of the street, and a gray and worn high school on the opposite side.

His Second Chance

At the next corner, we walked by a real estate office that plastered posters of all of the available listings in Boston on their windows. We stopped for a moment to study them, for fun. A $13 million Greek Revival from 1830 in Beacon Hill. An $8 million townhouse in Back Bay.

"Here's one in Hyde Park for $400,000," Tamara pointed out. "If we all put our money together, maybe we could afford that one?"

Living with two beautiful, albeit lesbian, women was every heterosexual man's dream. Despite my initial, embarrassing reaction to learning about their lifestyle, I was glad that Tamara easily accepted me.

We continued walking toward Queen Bee. We crossed Clarendon Street and cut into a narrow, red brick patio full of outdoor dining tables and portable heaters. Red and white patio umbrellas and giant oak trees shaded the patio. Happy hour patrons, accompanied by their dogs tethered to leashes, filled half of the seating areas. A hostess dressed in a black button-down shirt and black pants seated us at an outdoor table.

"Three glasses of Maker's Mark please," Maggie instructed the server a few minutes later. "Neat."

The waiter nodded in response and hustled away to get our drinks.

"How did you two meet anyway?" I leaned forward, resting my elbows on the wooden tabletop. The answer plagued me ever since I learned that Maggie and Tamara were a couple.

His Second Chance

"In the plumbing section of the hardware store," Tamara deadpanned. "Mags came up to me asking if she had the right parts and of course I said yes."

Both women howled in laughter.

I walked right into that one.

"If only it was that exciting," Maggie explained. "We met in a fine arts class senior year. We worked together on a project and the rest is history." She lovingly grabbed Tamara's hand.

Seeing Maggie happy with Tamara left me broken-hearted. My insides melted like ice cream left out in the hot sun. Maggie was my ice cream. My sweet chocolate chip. And now someone else lapped her up.

Even if I couldn't have Maggie in my bed, I still wanted her in my life. She didn't have the memories that I held of us talking for hours at a time, stealing kisses, and sharing food. Some days I forgot what I had for breakfast that morning, but I would always remember loving Maggie. She was part of me and always would be.

In a feeble attempt to mask my real feelings, I spoke, "You two are cute together."

"Aww, thanks," Tamara responded. "She's the love of my life."

Maggie blushed.

"How about you?" Maggie asked me. "Are you dating anyone? You always seemed to play the field when I knew you. Girls flocked to you like you had some kind of enchanting power. Like chocolate."

"Oh please," I scoffed. "That was not evident by the number of girls who agreed to go out with me. Present company included."

HIS SECOND CHANCE

"Well, I remember the few times we went out, girls always came up to you and flirted with you," Maggie explained. "I felt like a third wheel on *our* date."

Really? Is that why Maggie never believed I was serious about her? Is that why she switched teams and ended up with Tamara? I was a total fuckup. I didn't mean to make Maggie experience that. Maggie always made me believe I walked on air and maybe it trickled down to when I talked to other girls in front of her, even though I had zero interest in them.

"I'm sorry." Hurting Maggie was not my intention. "I shouldn't have made you feel like that. Those girls were just friends. I swear. I was young and stupid."

"Huh?" Maggie questioned. "That was only five years ago. It's not like you're forty now."

Oops. I needed to be more careful with my words. I knew I traveled back in time, but Maggie didn't. She thought I was in my mid-twenties, like her. My clothing and hair made me appear that age, but my mind knew otherwise. I wore baggy, khaki pants, a black T-shirt, and white sneakers. Most of my hair was still intact, but not as long as when I was in college because twenty-somethings shouldn't dress like poor college kids who can't afford to get a regular haircut.

"Oh, yeah, you're right," I stumbled. "Forty seems so *old*, doesn't it?"

Both girls chuckled at my ill attempt at humor. Crisis averted.

The three of us downed our bourbon and Tamara ordered us another round. Remembering that I didn't have much cash in my

HIS SECOND CHANCE

wallet, I was thankful that Tamara didn't expect me to pay because I was the guy.

We clinked our glasses in a toast and threw back the second shot of bourbon.

Maggie drunkenly nodded to Tamara like a bobblehead doll. She always was a lightweight. "I told Ryan he could bunk on my couch tonight."

Well if she insisted, I couldn't refuse a free place to stay. That solved part of my cash flow problem for the night.

"It's not like I have anything to worry about," Tamara jested.

"That is true!" Maggie concurred. She kissed Tamara on the mouth.

Did they not pay attention to me sitting right in front of them? Even if Maggie no longer found me attractive, that didn't mean that I didn't find her hot. I still wanted to take her ass in my hands, press her body against mine, and kiss her luscious lips. My nether regions tried to control themselves. God, she was so hot.

After two more rounds of Maker's Mark, the three of us shuffled out of Queen Bee, crossed the street, and found ourselves at an oyster bar. We ordered a dozen oysters and three oversized glasses of wine. I ordered a can of Jolt cola as a chaser. My stomach would not stay intact after the night's deluge of alcohol and food. But I didn't care.

After midnight, we headed back to Maggie's place, drunk and stumbling down the red brick sidewalk. As I tripped on an uneven brick and caught myself from doing a faceplant on the street, the girls whooped in laughter.

His Second Chance

"Did someone move the sidewalk?" I wagged a finger at it, accusing it of purposely trying to trip me.

The girls hugged a nearby tree in riotous laughter.

"Shh ... shh ... shh ..." I raised a crooked finger to my lips in an ill attempt to silence them. "We'll nake the weighbors."

"Did you say 'nake the weighbors?'" Tamara snickered.

"Noooo," Maggie interrupted, "he said 'take the vapors.'"

"What does *that* mean?" Tamara bellowed.

"I have NO idea!" Maggie cackled as she floundered down the sidewalk ahead of us. A nearby porch light sparked as the lightbulb burned out.

A few minutes later, Maggie managed to unlock her front door after she eyed it up a few times. The three of us stumbled up the stairs and spilled into her apartment, racing each other for the bathroom. Maggie shoved me aside and jumped ahead of Tamara and me.

"She's a fast little bugger," Tamara told me out of the side of her mouth. "No wonder I always had to chase her."

I chuckled realizing I wasn't the only one who pursued Maggie.

The last thing I remembered was sitting on the edge of Maggie's couch fumbling to take my shoes off.

HIS SECOND CHANCE

Chapter 11

"Dude!" Prashant called to me. "I've been searching for you everywhere. Why didn't you tell me you were guarding The Fence?"

"I ... What ... I ..." I sputtered, trying to quickly recognize my surroundings.

I found myself on a tattered brown couch a few feet away from Carnegie Mellon's concrete fence in the middle of campus between the College of Fine Arts and the School of Drama. Since 1923, students had painted The Fence to advertise their events. The School of Drama promoted their Playground Festival. The Student Dormitory Council invited students to come to The Fence to release their frustrations by screaming into the night during Primal Scream. Greek life advertised parties. Each group had to follow university rules of hand painting The Fence with the announcement between midnight and six a.m. No rollers or spray paints were allowed. Two members of the group had to guard The Fence round the clock in order to prevent other groups from painting over the message. Over

His Second Chance

six inches of paint helped land The Fence in the Guinness Book of World Records as The World's Most Painted Object.

Ring ... Ring ... Prashant's phone rang from his pocket.

"I thought you were helping me in the lab this afternoon?" Prashant asked me, ignoring his phone. "It's now after five and someone else has the lab scheduled." He appeared a little older than the last time I saw him when Maggie came to visit me in undergrad. He had gained a few pounds and he wore square, black-framed glasses instead of the round, wire-rimmed ones he had before.

Somehow, I traveled through time again.

What was happening to me? If Prashant was around 25, why was he still at CMU? Why was I back here? Would I see Maggie this time? Was she still with Tamara?

I inhaled a deep breath and stood from the couch, trying to present myself like I hadn't traveled through time again. Prashant could almost match the knowledge of Neil deGrasse Tyson, but I couldn't explain my journey to him yet because I didn't grasp the answers myself.

"Sorry, man, it completely slipped my mind," I fibbed. "I'm pretty sure I'm free tomorrow."

Ring ... Ring ... Prashant's phone rang again from his pocket and he made no attempt to reach for it.

"Aren't you answering that?" I asked him.

"No," he balked as he pushed his dark-framed glasses upward on his nose. "It's my mother. I know it. She's been calling me all day that she wants me to meet some girl. It's been a few years since Devya and I broke up and my mother thinks I'll waste away if I

His Second Chance

don't start dating again." Prashant rolled his eyes in annoyance. "Apparently, this new girl's family is pretty famous in India. No thanks."

Prashant ended up with Manju and they were perfect together. They both eschewed old-world tradition and wanted to do their own thing. I stood up for them when they eloped at the courthouse. For the life of me, I couldn't remember how they met.

"Your mother will keep calling you until you answer and agree to go on the date," I told him. "That's what they do."

"Yeah, I know," he sighed.

"What are your plans tonight?" I changed the subject, trying to get a grasp on what my purpose was in the here and now.

"I'm meeting some friends at PHI if you want to come along. Around ten. We heard some Pitt grad student girls will be there."

At least some things hadn't changed. PHI was the nickname for Panther Hollow Inn along Forbes Avenue. The dive bar was the unofficial middle-ground for Carnegie Mellon and Pitt students. I remembered getting $5 pitchers and $1 well drinks as a senior in undergrad. The odds were usually good that the female bartender was a frat boy's wet dream.

"Yeah, that'd be great," I told Prashant.

Ring ... Ring ... Prashant's phone rang for the third time.

"You gotta take that," I said. "She's gonna keep calling until you pick up."

Prashant harrumphed and shook his head in annoyance. In concession, he pulled the phone out of his pocket and flipped it open.

His Second Chance

"Hi, Mom," he answered, while rolling his eyes at me. "Okay, Mom ... Yes, Mom ... Okay, I'll meet her tonight ..."

He could barely get a word in edgewise. I smiled, sympathetic that my mom was the same way.

"Hold on a sec, Mom." He covered the mouthpiece of the flip phone with his hand and spoke to me, "Ryan, I gotta go, I'll see you at PHI later tonight."

"No prob," I replied and waved him off.

Prashant turned from me and took off down the sidewalk as I heard him say, "Okay, Mom, I'll meet her at seven ..."

The poor guy. I chuckled to myself, thankful that it wasn't me.

A few students scuttled on the pavement near me. Prashant said earlier it was after five, but what day was it? And year?

I wore a long-sleeved, light blue, denim button-down and jeans that I bought at Gap. The dry skies, cool temperatures, and multi-colored trees around me led me to believe that it was fall. Pushing the sleeve up on my shirt, I peered at my watch: "FR 2.10.98 5:22 p.m."

Friday, October 2, 1998. I skipped another three years. The first time I experienced 1998, I spent the previous two years getting my Master's at CMU. Why was I there again? Was three years a pattern? Or a random spot in time? Why was I jumping? How could I control where and when I jumped? Did each jump affect another? Where would I jump next? I had so many questions and still no answers.

Abandoning The Fence for the next group to promote their event, I shuffled down the sidewalk drowned in thought. I almost

HIS SECOND CHANCE

walked into the 20-foot green campus clock. Duh—I could have looked at it to tell me the time. But my watch provided the date.

A long string of empty water bottles decorated a nearby tree, compliments of the recycling club. Doherty Hall was to my left. I recognized it from my undergrad days, spending many days in the classrooms. As I wandered, I passed a few students on their bikes, ready for the weekend.

Why was I back at CMU? What was significant about the date?

Suddenly, a mobot buzzed within inches of my feet, nearly tripping me.

"What the hell ..." I glanced around, trying to scope out the controller of the mobile robot in my path.

A young kid, barely 18, came running up behind me holding a large remote control in his hands. He was skinny and unkempt, like I used to be. He reminded me a lot of my younger self.

"I'm so sorry! I'm so sorry!" he gasped, reaching down to pick up the rogue mobot from the pavement. "I hope it didn't clip you."

"Nah, you're good," I replied with a brush of my hand.

"Dr. Pausch wants us to get a leg up on our mobots, so I've been testing it out every day," the kid explained. "I'm getting it ready for the slalom race."

"It looks pretty good to me." I eyed his prototype. "Good luck."

"Thanks, man," he said. And he was off down the sidewalk.

The kid had me thinking. He said "Dr. Pausch ..."— of course! Randy Pausch was a professor in the Computer Science Department

His Second Chance

in 1998. Maybe he could help me. He came to Carnegie Mellon the semester after I graduated, so I never had the chance to meet him.

Dr. Pausch wrote one of my favorite books, *The Last Lecture,* in 2008. In the book, he boasted that he earned tenure faster than most professors because he often spent Friday nights in his office.

Only one way to find out.

HIS SECOND CHANCE

Chapter 12

As I ambled through the dimly lit halls of the Computer Science building searching for Randy Pausch's office, I gathered my thoughts. I couldn't blurt out that I traveled in time with an unknown plan. The good professor would surely laugh at me. I had to convince him that I was telling him the truth and wasn't a lunatic who wandered in off the street. After all, he was a scientist who needed facts.

Scenes of *Back to the Future* flashed in my head when Marty McFly first landed in 1955 and tried to convince Doc Brown who he was and where he came from.

A panel of light at the end of the hall caught my attention, adjourning my thoughts. Most of the other offices that I had passed were dark because those professors had gone home for the night to enjoy their weekends.

I jogged down the hall toward the light and decreased my pace as I approached the open door. The words "Randy Pausch, Ph.D."

His Second Chance

displayed across the glass. I gulped in a breath and knocked on the door.

"Dr. Pausch?"

"Yeah, come on in," a pleasant voice called.

As I stepped into his office, he eyed me suspiciously. He appeared 10 years younger than the author's picture on the cover of his book jacket: thick, dark hair, bushy eyebrows, and he wore a maroon CMU embroidered golf shirt.

"Do I know you?" he asked me. "You aren't in any of my classes."

"No, sir," I stated. I stroked my right hand where my scar used to be. Why was I so nervous? "My name is Ryan and I'm an undergrad-- no, I mean a grad student." No way would Randy Pausch believe that someone who dressed like he was in his late 20s was an undergrad.

"Are you sure about that?" he joked, obviously picking up on my stuttering.

"Yes, I *was* an undergrad here," I corrected myself, wiping my brow. "But now I'm a grad student." A slight fib wouldn't hurt anyone, would it? "And I wondered if you could help me?"

"Maybe." His mouth curved upward in a curious grin and he motioned to an empty chair. "Have a seat."

I exhaled and took a seat in the visitor's chair next to his desk. A collection of mini mobots congregated on his nearby shelves. Virtual reality prototype goggles took up space in the corner of the shelf. A white Disney name tag imprinted with "Randy" on it poked into a cork board.

His Second Chance

"I have a science problem and I don't have the answer," I explained.

"You gotta give me more than that," Randy Pausch chuckled. "That's this whole university."

"Okay ..." I gulped in another breath. "I can't explain it, but let me try a different approach."

He stared at me expectantly.

"Do you remember the movie *Back to the Future*?" I asked him, rubbing my right hand again where the scar should have been.

"Yes, of course. Good flick," he replied. "A few questionable logistics, but otherwise it was fun."

"Well, I'm Marty McFly," I explained. "Well, not *really* Marty McFly, but I'm traveling back in time like him."

Randy Pausch let out a loud belly laugh, one that came deep from within him, as if I told him the funniest thing he ever heard.

"You need to go find Doc Brown," he chuckled, trying to contain his laughter. He wiped a stray tear from his cheek, the aftermath of laughing so hard.

I didn't flinch.

"Oh, come on, you can't be serious!" Randy Pausch bellowed.

"I am, I swear," I stated. "One day I was in my mid-forties, then I was 21, then I was 24, and now I'm 27."

"You look 27 to me." He gestured to my twenty-something blue button-down and jeans. "Prove it to me. Tell me something about the future. Do we have driverless cars? Do we have an easier way to hail a taxi in this crazy city?"

His Second Chance

I wanted to tell him yes to both of those questions, but he would be unconvinced unless I provided him proof. I couldn't pull an Uber car out of my pocket to show him. Nor could I tell him that he would get married, have three kids, but not live to reach his 50th birthday. He would do a lot of remarkable things in the next ten years and I couldn't live with myself if I changed his life trajectory. Then I remembered reading something from the autobiography he had yet to write.

"You had a football coach when you were younger named Coach Graham," I explained. "He rode you pretty hard because he didn't give up on you even though you were the scrawniest kid on the team."

Randy Pausch's mouth fell open. "How could you possibly know that? Did you talk to my father?"

"Because you mention it in the future," I replied. I purposely stayed vague, so as not to alter his life. Doc Brown knew what he was talking about!

Randy Pausch stared at me unspeaking, as if his mouth tried to catch up with what his brain processed. He opened his mouth a few times and then closed it.

"I need your help. You have to believe me," I begged, breaking the deafening silence.

"How ... How does this work exactly?" he finally spoke, pointing a crooked finger at me as if he mentally tried to piece it all together.

"I don't know."

"What's happening?" Randy Pausch asked.

His Second Chance

"It's hard for me to explain. All I know is that I'm going to sleep and waking up at random points in my life and seeing things in a different path."

"Like what?"

"Like this girl, Maggie," I mused. "She and I dated in undergrad, but when we both graduated the first time around, she married someone else and then when I was in my late 30s, I found her on—" I stopped, realizing I couldn't disclose to Randy Pausch what Facebook was before it existed. "I mean, I found her again after 15 years and we caught up."

"Pretty normal stuff," he stated.

"But then a few years later, one night I was working at the physics lab here with my friend Prashant—"

"Prashant Kumar?" Randy Pausch interrupted me.

"Yeah, you know him?"

"He's one of my grad students. I saw him yesterday."

That piece of information might help explain why I was back at CMU now.

"Prashant and I were working in his chemistry lab and we must've miscalculated because something exploded and it knocked me out. I came to a few minutes later, but otherwise felt physically fine. Then the next day, I was walking down Forbes and a street lamp exploded above me."

"How does this girl Maggie fit in?" Randy Pausch wanted to know.

His Second Chance

"I was getting to that," I chuckled. "The morning after the street lamp exploded, I found myself back here, at CMU, as an undergrad, dating Maggie."

"That's good, right?"

"Yes," I answered. "I relived being myself at 21 again."

"Every man's dream," he chuckled. "And everyone else was the same? No one changed or knew anything different?"

"Correct," I replied.

"And you didn't run into your younger self?"

"No," I stated. "As far as I can tell, that isn't happening. But let me get back to Maggie." I raked a hand through my dark hair. "In the next jump, when I was 24, I landed in Boston and ran into Maggie and she was a lesbian. I met her girlfriend and everything. So, she didn't marry the original guy."

Randy Pausch stifled a laugh. "You turned a girl to the other team?"

"Yeah, don't remind me." I rolled my eyes. "Now I'm here in 1998. I think I'm in my mid-forties but my body says otherwise."

Randy Pausch leaned toward me, resting his elbows on his knees. "If I have this straight, you traveled in time, but don't have knowledge of how or why or when or what purpose you have in each of the jumps?"

"Yes."

"That's a lot of unanswered questions," he deduced.

"Tell me about it," I groaned.

"Wouldn't the time travel affect your DNA or molecular breakdown?" he asked me.

His Second Chance

"Possibly," I said, shaking my head. "I haven't witnessed any side effects."

"Is there a time differential?"

"I don't know the answer to that either," I sighed. "What if I do something now and it affects something else in the future? I'll grasp what is supposed to happen, but nobody else will. Like if I go back to the 60s and stop Lee Harvey Oswald from killing JFK, the whole world would be affected."

We both shuddered at the thought.

"I'm sorry that I don't have a lot of answers for you. I do a lot of computer science and programming, not molecular transitioning. My students study virtual reality and want to work on the next *Star Wars* film," Randy Pausch lamented. "My best advice is to keep to yourself and try not to affect anyone else. And let's hope you're not stuck here in 1998."

"Thank you. I appreciate it, Doc." I stood from my chair and took a few steps towards the door. "I wasn't sure if you could give me any answers or not, but I at least needed to get it off my chest and talk about it."

"No problem. Glad I could help." Randy Pausch followed me to the door. "Do me a favor. Find me again in twenty years and remind me that we had this conversation."

"Sure thing, Dr. Pausch," I lied. My heart hurt knowing that he would succumb to pancreatic cancer in ten years.

His Second Chance

Chapter 13

Ten minutes later, I wandered west down Forbes Avenue, leaving the campus behind me. The skyscrapers of downtown Pittsburgh sparkled three miles away as the moon pushed its way into the indigo evening sky. Cars hummed past me down the street. Weekend warriors strolled along the sidewalks searching for pubs.

The opulent Carnegie Museum of Natural History lit up the block across the street on my left. Founded by industrial entrepreneur and philanthropist Andrew Carnegie in 1896, its four elephantic marble columns supported the names Franklin, Bramante, and Phidias, paying homage to American polymath Benjamin Franklin, Italian architect and painter Donato Bramante, and Greek sculptor Phidias. Grand statues of Michelangelo and Galileo flanked the corners of the entrance, inviting science and art aficionados inside. Four marble light posts radiated the now-sleeping museum.

Even in the dark, the edifice cast a heavenly glow along the block. As I stopped in awe, taking in its glorious splendor, my

His Second Chance

stomach grumbled. If I remembered correctly, Union Grill was around the corner on South Craig Street. I wasn't meeting Prashant for another few hours, so I had some time to kill—as long as I had enough cash in my pocket.

I backtracked Forbes Avenue toward South Craig and paused at the stoplight to cross the intersection. As other pedestrians waited across the street for the same signal, one of them caught my attention: a young woman with dark hair and cocoa skin. She wrapped herself in an oversized multi-colored sweater and focused her attention downward, away from the crowd. From across the street, she looked familiar to me. Was she who I thought she was?

I couldn't will the light to change fast enough so that I could cross the street to figure out if the woman was who I thought she was. Her puffy eyes and saddened face made me think that she had been crying.

More cars whizzed by in front of me, preventing me from jaywalking to reach her and console her. Hopefully, she would accept solace from me.

Finally, the traffic switched direction and I crossed the street. While I strode across the intersection, the young woman must have remembered something and turned the opposite way and headed down the sidewalk. I batted my way through oncoming pedestrians trying to reach her. A man walking his dog tripped me in the process. In the moment that I focused on the dog so that I wouldn't fall to the pavement, the young woman was gone when I finally glimpsed up again.

"Manju?" I pondered.

His Second Chance

* * * *

After three hours of nursing a couple of $5 Copper Mug Mules at Union Grill and noshing on a chophouse burger, I headed out the door to meet Prashant at Panther Hollow Inn around the corner.

A hefty, red awning covered glass windows full of neon beer signs on the PHI frontage. I pushed in the oak door and stepped inside. A noxious smog of cigarette smoke knocked me off my feet. Unfortunately for me, the state smoking ban in public places wouldn't take effect for another ten years.

Bar patrons filled the wooden booths along the left wall. More clientele packed in all the spaces at the bar. I could barely see through the crowd. I ordered a Vodka Red Bull and continued the hunt for my friend.

"Ryan!" Prashant's voice called me from the back. His arm reached up and beckoned me.

"Hey, man," he said to me and motioned to two other guys standing near him with bottles of Rolling Rock in their hands. "This is Chad and Damien. They work in the lab with me."

"Good to meet you," I replied as they nodded in acknowledgment.

"You too, man," Chad replied.

"How was your date?" I turned to Prashant with a wide grin. "When's the wedding?"

"Never," he replied. "She bailed."

"What?" I balked. "That's not cool."

His Second Chance

Prashant scoffed in agreement. "My mother kept going on and on about this girl Ju and she couldn't even bother to show up. Screw her."

Ju? Short for Manju? If it was her, why did they not meet? She obviously couldn't text him to say why she didn't show up. Not while I was in 1998.

Prashant and Manju were supposed to be together. Their story kept me centered. If they didn't start dating, it was somehow my fault. It had to be. I wondered if my time travel affected other people. I could never live with myself if they didn't get married.

Randy Pausch's prophecy might come true.

If that was Manju I saw on the street earlier, why was she crying? Something must have happened that she and Prashant didn't meet. If they don't meet, Taj and Gia will never be born. If their kids are never born, neither one will have a reason to stay in Pittsburgh where I would eventually bunk at their house. And if I don't visit them, I might never get back to my mid-forties where the lab explosion happened, causing me to jump in the first place. I gulped at the thought. The endless circle of questions made me dizzy. I needed to get Prashant and Manju together, but how?

I shuddered at the thought that I might be stuck in 1998 again. No smartphones. No Uber. No Facebook or Amazon. I couldn't hint to anyone that the Y2K panic was a bust. Unfortunately, I'd have to live through 9/11 again. And no one would believe me that Donald Trump would eventually be president.

A green neon Rolling Rock sign shattered on the bar wall, breaking me from my contemplation.

His Second Chance

Chapter 14

The next morning, I awoke at the Paul Revere Statue plaza in Boston again.

What was going on? Why did I keep traveling between Pittsburgh and Boston? Would I ever run into myself? So far I hadn't, so I was safe. I hated that I couldn't take the reins of my fate. But was someone else controlling it or was something I did affecting the time of events? I had to figure it all out. And soon.

I stood from the brick bench and checked my watch: "TU11. 3. 3. 7:47 a.m."

Tuesday, March 11, 2003.

Because of the cooler temperatures, only a handful of tourists in spring jackets braved the elements to snap pictures of the early American patriot. I exited the plaza and faced Hanover Street again. Instead of heading right like I did the last time, a feeling inside nudged me left, deeper into the North End of the city.

As I rounded a patch of trees adjacent to the sidewalk, the Ladder No. 1 Fire Department stood, tranquil, to my left. Cars whirred passed me along the street. A few produce vans followed the

95

His Second Chance

cars, delivering fresh goods to the local restaurants and markets. More cars and small trucks parked along the curb.

As I waited at the edge of the intersection for traffic to lessen, a woman across the street accompanying two young children caught my attention. The older child, a girl with golden curls down her back, grasped the woman's hand and skipped down the cement path. She appeared old enough to be in kindergarten with her purple unicorn backpack. The brown-haired boy, a few inches shorter than his sister, scurried off down the sidewalk in search of rocks. His navy blue, open jacket flapped in the breeze as he squatted down, examining his finds.

The woman's profile prevented me from seeing her entire face. She wore a tan trench coach, belted at the waist. Her blonde hair was pulled back into a low ponytail that hugged her neck. She and the little girl stopped as they caught up to the boy who was occupied with a handful of rocks he discovered. The woman gestured for the boy to stand so that she could zip up his jacket.

I never had kids; encountering them was pure joy and amusement for me.

Then a man with a small dog on a leash postponed my thoughts. He was tall and had a head of dark hair.

"Maggie!" he called to her, chasing after her down the sidewalk with a lidded, white, foam cup in his hand. "You forgot your coffee, babe." The little brown and white dog, a mix between a corgi and a beagle, yipped at his feet. The pooch wore a blue dog vest.

Oh my god. Maggie. My Maggie.

His Second Chance

I frantically searched to my left and to my right, trying to find a place to hide. She couldn't see me. I wanted to observe her from afar first before—and if—I decided to make my presence known. Quickly, I ducked behind a black pickup truck parked in the alley next to me. Slowly, I inched around the side, keeping most of my body hidden while I viewed the scene in front of me.

Maggie turned to face the man. "Thanks, honey," she said and kissed him on the mouth. When he gingerly touched her face with his palm, a gold band sparkled on his left hand.

Whoa.

I slunk behind the truck, completely out of sight. The last time I spent time with Maggie, she swapped spit with Tamara and called her the love of her life.

I quickly did the math in my head. Seven years had passed. What happened in those seven years? Maggie now had children. And a husband. How did her life take another drastic turn? As hard as it was, I had come to grips with her being a lesbian, leaving her unavailable to me. But now this changed everything again. And what happened to Tamara?

I turned back to face the charming family. My eyes narrowed, focusing on Maggie's husband. He looked familiar to me. Where had I seen him before?

"Have a great day at work, babe," he told her, grasping her waist with his hand.

As he smiled at her, she lovingly poked a finger at the dimple in his cheek. "You're so cute."

His Second Chance

I gasped as I realized how I recognized him. What was his name? The guy from the fraternity party when I jumped back to being a junior at Carnegie Mellon. When I first met him, I didn't think twice about him. He was a blip in my existence. What was his name? Martin? No. Marshall? No, that wasn't it either. Mavsomething. That's right. Maverick. I mean Brett. Maggie met him for the first time that night too. How did *they* get together? They met each other for what, an hour at that party? She was supposed to be with me, not him. Jealousy boiled inside me.

Brett kissed Maggie again, then squatted down and pecked each of their children on their rosy cheeks. His son proudly showed his dad his new findings in his small hand and Brett beamed with joy.

"Have a great day, Madelyn," Brett told his daughter. "I'll see you after school."

"Thanks, Daddy," the little girl gushed as she hugged him. She patted the small dog on the head. "See you later, Rocky. I'll miss you."

Brett stood again to face his wife and handed her the coffee. He kissed Maggie again and said, "I love you."

"I love you, too." She smiled widely at him, pausing a few extra moments taking him in. "Now I gotta run or Madelyn and Thomas will be late for school."

Brett shooed them off and turned the opposite way, with Rocky the dog, scurrying at his feet.

Maggie and her kids shuffled down the sidewalk, happy and at ease.

His Second Chance

I slunk behind the truck again, my head in my hands. This whole time-travel fucked with me. I had the opportunity to do things differently in my life, but at what cost to others? I thought I had been given the opportunity to make changes in my life, but maybe that wasn't the case.

Maggie had radiance and I couldn't mess with that. She always wanted a family and her two beautiful children gave her that wish. Her husband obviously adored her if he rushed after her to make sure she had her coffee for the day. She appeared happy and in love with him.

If I interrupted Maggie's wondrous life, she might resent me because she might miss out on so many amazing things and it would be my fault. I believed I could simply hit a redo button with this time traveling and everything would be okay. The first time around, I failed to commit to Maggie, and I wanted to redeem myself. That could have been the single crossroads in my life that might have changed everything. But now I can't. I won't.

What was the core thread linking all of these events in my life? If I changed one thing, did it have a ripple effect to another time? Did the concept of multiple universes dictate that only one instance of every consciousness could exist? Where did the prior consciousness go once I jumped? Would I jump into the future and find myself an old, cantankerous bastard? The questions plagued me.

The only answer I knew was that Maggie was the love of my life. She gave me strength. She calmed me. She was my safe haven in the chaos of where I would wake up next. No matter what happened, she would always burn sweet memories in my heart. I wanted her to find happiness, even if it wasn't with me.

On our first date, we spent hours talking and laughing over burgers and French fries, then finished the night making out in the alcoves of the Fine Arts building on campus. Before her, I never would have dreamed about kissing someone like that on a first date. I didn't find my confidence until Maggie came into my life.

She was the most beautiful person in the world to me. I found myself in her, even though I was too much of a dumbass to tell her how much I loved and needed her when I graduated from college. Had I told her, things might have been different. She should have been kissing *me* on the sidewalk and chatting with *our* kids.

If I couldn't have her now, I hoped that we would meet up again so that I could tell her I had traveled through time to witness many changes in my life. She was my home.

Suddenly, a bolt of lightning assaulted me out of my thoughts. Rain pellets showered down in succession. I frantically viewed my surroundings for cover and located a black awning across the street at the entrance of a corner deli.

Dodging a few oncoming cars, I bolted across the street as the rain soaked me. I snuck into the cafe taking protection from the rain.

"What can I get for you?" the clerk asked me.

"Um ... I ... " I quickly perused the overhead menu, realizing that I needed to place an order as a common courtesy for using the deli as a safe haven. "A Monster energy drink."

His Second Chance

The clerk rang up my order and I pulled three ragged dollar bills out of my pocket and handed them to him.

I cracked open the can and sipped on it, studying the rain pummeling down the exterior of the window.

After five minutes in shelter, the rain subsided enough that I wouldn't get soaked if I ventured out. I pushed the cafe shop door open and stepped onto the narrow sidewalk.

A new bolt of lightning struck a metal street lamp above me, sending shards of glass and metal into the street around me. I didn't have time to protect myself.

Then everything went black.

HIS SECOND CHANCE

Chapter 15

I awoke to find myself in a bedroom I didn't recognize. In a dark haze provided by the beginnings of sunrise through the blinds, I made out a wooden dresser and a second-hand night stand. Nothing was on the walls. The bed I slept in did not have a headboard or a bed frame. A small door on the interior wall of the room led to a closet.

Where was I?

I stumbled out of the bed, knocking a lumpy, dark green comforter to the floor. Realizing I only wore boxer briefs, I scratched my partially hairy chest and peeked into my drawers. Hmmm. I had recently done some manscaping. My watch was not on my wrist so I had no idea what year it was, but I assumed I was older because I had put on a few pounds. Without proof in a mirror of my image, I rubbed a hand across my stubble-laden face.

I opened the closet door and found a gray sweatshirt hung from an interior hook. Finding my pants, I shrugged both on and opened

His Second Chance

the door to the hallway. Out of habit, I patted my back pocket to make sure my wallet was still there. It was.

Prashant found me in the hall, sipping a cup of coffee. "Oh good, you're up. We accomplished a lot last night. How's your head?" The dark beard on his face matched the erratic hair on his head. A few wrinkles outlined tired eyes behind his dark framed glasses. He wore holey, black sweatpants, a gray, threadbare T-shirt that somehow survived two decades, and a ratty robe. On his feet, he wore once-white sweat socks and rubber flip-flops.

By Prashant's older, wrinkled, and gray features, I guessed I was back in the present.

"It's fine." I patted the back of my head and touched a small lump where I hit the floor in the lab. So much had happened to me lately, that I forgot I smacked my head off the floor after the lab explosion.

Even though Prashant was a welcome sight, I was still unsure of where I was. Probably his house. But nothing looked familiar. "Is Manju in the kitchen?"

"Who?"

"Manju. Your wife." I stared him down with narrowed eyes.

"Dude, what the hell are you talking about?" Prashant volleyed. "What wife?"

His bare left hand held the coffee cup. Oh no. Something happened in the course of the changed time continuum that he and Manju never got married. Then they never had Taj and Gia. What did I do? Panic filled me as I tried to think of how to fix this. I

His Second Chance

feverishly scraped the back of my neck trying to knead out the new anxiety.

"Oh, right, what was I thinking? I guess I had a weird dream that you were married," I lied.

I followed as Prashant dragged himself down the hall to the kitchen. We were in his restored brick row home in North Oakland again, but the place didn't seem the same. No little kids laughing and talking, begging for their parents' attention. No toys strewn everywhere. No sweet smells of Manju's cooking filling the air. The large print of the Hyderabad temples hung crooked on the dingy white wall.

What did I do?

Prashant pulled a coffee cup from an overhead cabinet, sniffed it, then handed it to me. As he reached up, I took notice of the black tattoo on his forearm. At least that ink hadn't changed.

"I think it's clean," he said. "Help yourself." He pointed to the 1980-esque coffee maker gurgling on the counter to his left, belching out its near-last breath. Manju would have insisted on a Keurig. She always kept everything organized and tidy in their household.

I poured myself a cup of coffee, fingering a few grounds out of the mug.

Without Manju and his kids, Prashant was now a codger without the deep wrinkles and gray beard. He was in his mid-40s, but shuffled around the kitchen like his bones ached. His change concerned me. But now that he had never met Manju, how would he realize what he missed?

His Second Chance

I took a seat at his sticky kitchen table which was covered with random crumbs. Manju would have been horrified at the crud.

"Prashant," I spoke as delicately as I could, "you and I have been best friends for a long time. We need to talk."

"You sound like the last girl who broke up with me," he interrupted, taking a swig of his coffee.

"Um, okay." My mind raced trying to come up with a way to not sound like I was his ex. The direct approach inched its way forward. He might not believe me, but that was the chance I had to take. "I have something to tell you."

Prashant stared at me expectantly.

How would I explain that I had traveled through time and affected his life without telling him that the life he had now was not supposed to happen?

"Well?" Prashant took a swig of his coffee, interrupting my thoughts.

"Sorry." I shook my head and gulped in a deep breath. "I traveled through time," I blurted.

"Dude, you must've sniffed too many vapors in the lab last night," Prashant scoffed.

"I think that's how it all started," I pondered out loud. "With the blast."

"How what all started?"

"Traveling in time," I stated. "That's what I'm trying to tell you."

"You fucking with me?" Prashant scoffed.

His Second Chance

"No, I swear." My mind raced as I tried to come up with a way to prove it to him. I dug my wallet out of my back pocket and pulled out my driver's license.

"Look, my ID doesn't expire until 2023," I stated.

"Nice try," Prashant volleyed. "That's what mine says too, dumbass."

I puffed out an exasperated sigh. I pillaged through the rest of my wallet and found an old, wrinkled picture of Prashant, Manju, and me taken in grad school at Spring Carnival at CMU. "Here, what about this?" I asked him.

"Yeah, that's you and me ... and some girl I've never seen before. Why'd you Photoshop her in?" He gripped his cup of coffee in his hand, ready to take a sip.

Convincing Prashant would be harder than I expected. I focused on something he told me he experienced without me but nothing specific came to mind. We had shared a lot of great times in undergrad and grad school, but he would have also remembered the memories. I kneaded my right hand where my scar should have been. Even though I was in the present, the scar on my right hand had disappeared!

Then the answer hit me.

"Remember that girl Devya you dated in undergrad?" I declared.

"Yeah, what about her?" Prashant answered, taking another sip of his coffee. "I haven't talked to her in years."

"She was the first girl you kissed."

CRASH!

His Second Chance

The coffee mug slipped out of Prashant's hand and shattered on the kitchen table, sending broken shards of ceramic and random streams of hot java everywhere.

He and I jumped from the table, grabbed some tattered dish towels, and started sopping up the mess.

"How ... How ... the hell did you know that?" Prashant stuttered. "I never told anyone that."

"Because you told me, er, your *wife* told me," I explained. "Here in this kitchen, but in an alternate present."

"An alternate present?" Prashant repeated. "You're fucking with me."

"Yes, that's what I'm trying to tell you," I pleaded. "I traveled back in time and now I'm in the present again. And you don't have a wife this time."

Prashant blew out a sigh and chuckled. "Okay, let's say I humor you, how can you prove to me that you traveled in time?"

My mind searched for answers. Every time I jumped, Prashant had the same memories. But I had no proof of Manju.

"I ... I can't ..." I stuttered. "All I know is that I went back to 1992 when we lived on Beeler, then I jumped to 1995 in Boston, then 1998 back at CMU and 2003 to Boston again, and now I'm back here."

Prashant shook his head trying to keep up with me.

"I get why you were at CMU in 1992 and 1998, but why did you go to Boston?" he inquired.

"Because of Maggie," I replied.

His Second Chance

"Maggie? Kevin's sister Maggie?" Prashant wanted to know. "The one you dated in college? The cute blonde from Penn?"

"Yeah, Kevin's sister." Prashant, Kevin, and I had kept in touch over the years through Facebook and Instagram.

"I didn't know you still contacted her," Prashant stated.

"Yeah, I found her on Facebook years ago and we started talking again," I replied. I didn't want to let on that Maggie and I talked several times a month. Prashant might think it was weird.

"When was the last time you saw her?"

"Yesterday," I replied.

"Yesterday?" Prashant countered. "No way. You were with me yesterday."

"That's what I'm trying to tell you. Something happened after the lab explosion. Then when I went to Hemingway's to get burgers for you and—" I stopped myself, realizing that I was about to say *Manju* and Prashant wouldn't recognize her name. Convincing Prashant that I traveled in time was hard enough. No way would he believe me that he was married with two kids. "—me. While I was there, a street lamp exploded above me."

"And you think this is what caused you to travel back in time?" Prashant connected the dots.

"I don't know? Maybe? It's the only thing that makes sense."

Prashant stared at me as the gears churned inside his head. "Let's think about this. What have we learned about time travel?"

"Not much, except in the movies," I lamented.

"Exactly," Prashant confirmed. "In *Terminator*, a robotic super-assassin that resembles a real human is sent back in time to

His Second Chance

preemptively kill the future leader of the human resistance in a robot war."

I nodded as he paced around the small, dirty kitchen.

Prashant continued, thinking out loud, "Then there's *Star Trek 4, Hot Tub Time Machine, Captain America*, and, of course, *Back to the Future*."

"Sometimes I feel like Marty McFly," I muttered.

"Each one of those has a consistent mode of transportation, like the DeLorean or the hot tub. What's your mode?"

"I don't have one," I replied. "I go to sleep in one year and wake up the next morning in another."

"But you've been to these cities before," Prashant deduced. "Of course, you were in Pittsburgh for college and you told me you often traveled to Boston for work."

"That makes sense," I said. "I have been given the opportunity to redo previous times in my life."

"But how do you get there?" Prashant begged the question.

"Well, when I left Boston *yesterday*, a lightning bolt hit a street lamp above me and then everything went black," I explained. "Then I woke up here, in the present."

"Something is happening with the jolts of electricity near you," Prashant concluded. He pondered a moment. "Do you have any idea where you'll end up when you jump?"

"Not a clue," I said.

"It's like you're Mahakaal," Prashant stated.

"Who?"

His Second Chance

"Mahakaal means someone who is supreme and above the time-period or the boundaries of time," Prashant explained. "It's a Hindu thing. My parents forced it on me when I was a kid."

"You mean like Hermes, the Greek god?" I asked him. "I learned about him in Mythology class in high school. He was the god of travel, trade, luck, wealth, thieves, and language and viewed as the protector and patron of roads and travelers."

"Yes, it's similar. You're like Hermes, that's for sure," Prashant chuckled. "Maybe that's what we need to call my project. The Hermes Experiment."

"That works. I might need some wings on my shoes for all the flying I'm doing," I joked.

"Is there anything that has changed since you traveled?" Prashant hiked up his sagging, holey sweatpants. "Because if there is, you need to go back and fix it."

My stomach dropped.

His Second Chance

Chapter 16

"Yes," I stated. "I need to go back. I need to find Maggie again."

What I told Prashant wasn't exactly a lie, but I couldn't tell him yet that I affected *his* life. I couldn't figure out what I did to change his course. Did I crush a butterfly somewhere?

"Okay, then we need to recreate the explosion."

* * * *

Fifteen minutes later, we were back at the campus lab. In Prashant's time frame, we were there 12 hours before, but in mine, it was a lifetime ago. He had cleaned up the lab, erasing any evidence of the explosion that knocked me out the day before.

"What date do you want to go back to?" Prashant wanted to know.

I quickly did the math in my head. Prashant and Manju were supposed to meet in early October 1998, so I had to jump back to that same timeframe.

His Second Chance

"Let's go with October 1st, 1998," I told him. He didn't need to be aware that I didn't see Maggie at that time. My priority was getting Prashant back together with Manju; Maggie could wait. For now.

"It's not like we can set a calendar on the dashboard of a car," Prashant explained, "so our best bet is to will the date as best we can. Clear your head and concentrate on that date."

Pursing my lips together, I vacated every other notion in my mind focusing on October 1st, 1998. God, I hoped it worked.

Prashant and I spent the next hour fusing lithium hydroxide and hydrofluoric acid in the heat sealer to recreate the explosion.

"Is it working?" Prashant and I leaned over the lip of the cylinder, examining the amalgamation. "How will we know?"

"I think—" Prashant started to say.

BANG!

Molecular fireballs sputtered out of the container into a small cloud hovering atop the metal counter, paling in comparison to the first time. Prashant and I jumped back in anticipation of an aftershock, but nothing came.

"That's it? Seems anticlimactic, doesn't it?" I wondered out loud.

"I did everything the same," Prashant replied. "At least I'm pretty sure I did. Sorry, man."

We gawked at the now simmering cylinder. Inside it, blue and red particles fizzled down into solid specks.

His Second Chance

"But what about the street light explosion?" I inquired. "That added to it."

"I can't recreate that," Prashant sighed. "It's not like in *Back to the Future* where we can plan when a street lamp will explode."

"True." I frowned, disappointed that we couldn't come up with a solution.

I might be stuck in the present this time, unable to go back and fix Prashant's love life. I would never forgive myself if he couldn't meet Manju.

A half hour later, Prashant and I ambled up to the lacquered bar at Hemingway's, still down about our failed experiment.

"What do you want to drink?" I asked him. "My treat."

"Just a Red Bull," he said. "I'm not in the mood for beer."

I raised a finger toward the bartender to get her attention. "Two Red Bulls, please."

HIS SECOND CHANCE

Chapter 17

The next morning, I awoke in the same beige, box apartment far off campus from Carnegie Mellon where I lived while attending grad school—in 1999. I glanced out the window as cars and buses rumbled along Fifth Avenue and turned onto Shady Avenue. Snow-covered grass surrounded the apartment buildings. Someone had built a snowman in the postage stamp yard across the street.

"What the hell?" I uttered to myself. "How did I get here? Prashant's experiment didn't work."

My cell phone rang from atop my dresser.

I stumbled out of bed, reached for it, and flipped it open.

"Hello?"

"Hey, man, where are you?!" Prashant reprimanded me. His high volume made me deduce he was not happy.

"In my room," I answered, giving the best response I could muster. Obviously, it was winter, but I had no idea what month or year it was until I examined my watch, which was not on my right wrist.

His Second Chance

"You were supposed to be here ten minutes ago," Prashant scolded me.

"And here is ... ?" I cringed, knowing full well that his annoyance meter would reach its max in the next ten seconds.

"What the fuck, man?!" Prashant yelled. Make it two seconds. "We've had plans for a week now. If you don't get your ass over here in the next fifteen minutes, I'll do this lab without you and you can fail."

Click.

Oops. Somehow, I pissed off Prashant.

A lab? That narrowed it down a little bit. What kind of lab would Prashant be in while I was in grad school? If I didn't figure it out in the next few minutes, he would have my ass.

I grabbed my watch from my dresser, wrapped it around my wrist, and studied it at the same time: "WE24. 2.99 9:51 a.m."

Wednesday, February 24, 1999.

If my memory served me right, it took a good half hour to walk to campus from my grad school apartment. I needed to double-time it so I didn't piss off Prashant any more than he already was.

Twenty minutes later, I huffed into Hamerschlag Hall, kicking snow off my boots and unzipped my parka. Winter in Pittsburgh was brutal. The bone-chilling wind charged down the streets, forcing those who dared to venture out to walk with one hand covering their face and the other holding their hat on their head.

"You had two more minutes and I was outta here." Prashant glared at me with daggers for eyes.

His Second Chance

"I'm sorry, man," I told him, pulling a knit beanie off my head. "I fell asleep."

For the next two hours, Prashant and I worked in the chem lab, nose-deep in aromatic hydrocarbons.

My stomach grumbled in revolt because I hadn't paid attention to it in several hours.

"Let's get some lunch." I rubbed my groaning belly. "I'm starving."

"Good idea," Prashant said, his tone softening from the morning. "I could eat something."

We grabbed our winter jackets and hoofed through the snow to Margaret Morrison Street and found Sree's food van parked at the curb. Despite the low-rent image of the dented old vehicle, Prashant and I frequented this place for the $4 tamarind chicken platter.

An Indian lady, who was short enough to fit into the open trunk of the van, served us our piping hot food. We snatched the steaming foil platters from her and raced over to the University Center to sit indoors and eat.

Inside the Cohon Center, we snagged an empty black couch in the three-story atrium. Other students shuffled by us in their snow gear, possibly heading to the meeting rooms, the generous selection of lunch choices on the second floor, or the fitness center.

"What are you doing after this?" I forked my chicken and took a bite.

"I don't know," Prashant uttered. "Going back to the lab."

"Do you still need me?"

"Nah, I'm good for now," Prashant replied.

His Second Chance

In a trance, I gazed at the steady flow of students coming in and out of the atrium. "I think I'll stick around here for a little while." I grasped that I was back in my Master's program, but why? I needed to spend more time on my own to figure it out.

Prashant finished his lunch and gathered up his trash. "I'll see you back at the apartment later tonight."

"Sure thing, bro."

And he was gone.

Even though my chicken filled me, I was in the mood for something sweet. I climbed the stairs two by two, bypassing other students taking their time. On the second floor, a cafe with a display of cookies and muffins caught my eye.

"I'll take a chocolate chip cookie," I said to the clerk as I reached for my college ID in my back pocket. Hopefully, the stripe still worked for me to swipe a snack.

As I waited with bated breath for the sweet sound of success, a female voice behind me said, "Those things always have a mind of their own. I never know if mine will work or not."

I turned around and came face-to-face with the owner.

Manju.

Chapter 18

Stunned to come opposite her, I could barely utter anything. "I ... uh ... I ..."

"You sure can charm the ladies," Manju joked, obviously taking notice of my shock. She shouldered past me to pay for her blueberry muffin but turned her body toward me to maintain our conversation. "I'm Manju."

The combination of her boldness and her lack of knowledge of who I was floored me. Of course, she wouldn't recognize me. She hadn't met Prashant yet.

"I'm ... I'm ... Ryan," I finally spoke, still processing how to present myself to her.

"Yeah, I know." She nodded to the cookie in my hand. "Do you want to join me?"

Of course, I did; I needed to figure out how to introduce her to Prashant and fix his love life.

"Uh... yeah, that'd be cool."

His Second Chance

She sauntered past me and found an empty table in the center of the food court. I took a seat across from her. Then it finally dawned on me what she said.

"How do you know me?" I asked, glaring sideways at her.

"You're in my data mining for decision-making class," she replied matter of factly, grazing my arm with her fingers. "You sit a few rows over from me." She unzipped her jacket, revealing a top that exposed the skin of her chest. Manju leaned into the table, obviously making herself comfortable. With a flick of her long dark hair, she smiled at me.

"Where's your girlfriend?" Manju casually looked behind me as if she waited for someone to join me.

Hey, that was my line when I wanted to find out a girl's relationship status. The answer was either that she didn't have one or that her boyfriend was at such and such a place. Nice play, Manju, nice play.

"I ... I ... don't have one."

"Oh, come on," she purred, "surely a guy like you has a girlfriend." Her lips curved upward into a sensuous smile.

My mouth fell open. If I didn't know any better, Manju was flirting with me. But she couldn't be. She shouldn't be! She was supposed to marry Prashant and have kids with him. I considered Taj and Gia my niece and nephew.

"I don't," I said. My insides wrestled, realizing a pretty girl was feeding my ego, but grasped that Manju was not the one for me. Maggie was, even though she was somewhere else in time. I couldn't, wouldn't, bite the tempting hook that Manju dangled.

His Second Chance

Manju nibbled at her cookie and stared me down over the top of her hand. "Well ... since you don't have a girlfriend, maybe you'd like to join me for drinks tomorrow night?"

I chomped at my cookie and gulped it down. I didn't want to turn her down for fear of not getting her together with Prashant. But I didn't want to lead her on either.

"Um, yeah, that'd be great," I replied.

"Wanna meet me at PHI around 7:00 tomorrow?" she offered.

"Yeah, that works," I mumbled.

Manju quickly glanced at her watch. "Sorry, but I gotta run. I gotta go meet someone." She stood from the table and disappeared into the crowd.

What just happened? Somehow, I agreed to a date with Manju. I wiped my brow and blew out a heavy sigh. What would I do? I had one day to figure out how to make her lose interest in me and introduce Prashant to her at the same time, assuming and hoping that I didn't jump through time again.

I stood from the table and exited the food court, heading down the stairs to the first floor.

As I wove my way around other students, a professor heading to the auditorium caught my attention.

"Dr. Pausch!" I called to him.

He turned and stopped, trying to figure out who, in the mass of students in the surrounding area, shouted his name.

"It's me, Ryan." I jogged over to him, closing the gap between us. "Do you remember how I stopped in your office—" I quickly did the math in my head, trying to remember when I last

His Second Chance

encountered him in his lifetime "—in the fall and told you about traveling in time?" Maybe he could give me some insight on how to reconnect Prashant and Manju?

"Oh yeah, I remember." He confirmed with a head nod. "Where have you been this time? In the future battling four-headed aliens?"

"Ha ha, no," I chuckled, leaning into him trying to make sure no one could hear our conversation. "But I have a problem."

"What happened? Did you crush a butterfly somewhere?" Randy Pausch inquired.

"I ... I ... must have ..." I wiped my brow as beads of sweat formed. "I messed up somewhere and I don't know how. I was so careful. I guarantee I was."

"Tell me," he pushed. "Maybe I can help you backtrack it."

"It's Prashant," I explained. "Pardon my French, but I fucked up. Originally, he was a happily married guy who had a couple of rugrats running around. But now, in my present, he's a cranky, sloppy bachelor hiking up holey sweatpants who's only interested in his work."

"Hey! You described *me* on the weekends!" Randy Pausch shot back with a broad grin.

"But he isn't *supposed* to be like that." I shook my head in bewilderment. "I did something and I don't know what it was."

"Then fix it," Randy Pausch replied. "You're a smart guy. Take every ounce of your being, figure it out, and fix it."

"You're right, Dr. Pausch," I said.

I knew exactly what I had to do.

HIS SECOND CHANCE

Chapter 19

At 6:55 the next night, I pushed through the door of PHI. Compared to the weekend crowd, the drinking congregation was sparse for a Thursday night. A few people filled the green vinyl booths that had been there since the 70s. An overhead fan propelled the stale beer stench. A few inebriated regulars claimed vacancy at the wooden bar. A catchy song by the Barenaked Ladies blared from overhead speakers.

Noticing that Manju hadn't come yet, I took a seat at the far end of the bar, saving an empty barstool next to me.

"What can I get for you, sweetie?" A perky bartender approached me, pressing her hands onto the top of the lacquered bar. Her tight, white Budweiser T-shirt barely contained her ample chest. I bet she earned a lot of tips.

"Can I get a Jager Bomb?" I asked. She turned and made my drink while I waited for Manju.

His Second Chance

A minute later, the fetching bartender placed two glasses in front of me: a shot glass of Jägermeister and a pint glass half-filled with Red Bull. "Here you go. Do you want to start a tab?"

"No, I'll pay cash," I told her, still hesitant that my future credit cards wouldn't work. I reached in my wallet and handed her a twenty-dollar bill I had borrowed from Prashant earlier in the day.

I picked up the shot glass and dropped it into the pint glass. In an instant, the two liquids fused into a creamy foam, inching up the side of the glass.

"I could give you a better lift than that," a female voice behind me whispered close to my ear.

Holy crap! I twisted my body around to find out who had said something so ballsy.

"Manju!" Had those words come from any other woman, I would have been flattered and ready to take her home. My mind wandered at the notion of finding out exactly what she meant. But reality shook me back to earth. My goal was to get Manju together with Prashant, at the sacrifice of my own netherregions.

"Hi, Ryan," she purred. Manju wore skin-tight jeans, a cropped leather jacket with a deep-cut tank top underneath, and fuck-me heels. Thank god I was sober, otherwise I might have fallen prey to her. She could have lured me like a siren and I never would have made it back to the surface. I would die a quick death if someone else wore something like that for me. But this was Manju. I had to keep my senses about me.

"You look great," I told her with a smile. Mental head slap. What was I thinking? I couldn't compliment her nor eye her up.

His Second Chance

"Thank you." She motioned to my drink and bit on her lower lip. "Mind if I join you? We could get wasted on these and see where the night takes us. Maybe have a little fun later."

Pointing to the empty seat next to me for her to sit, I laughed nervously. Wow, she laid it on thick. I chugged my drink in a feeble attempt to figure out what to say next.

"Do I make you nervous?" Manju stared at me like I was her animal caught in a trap and she was ready to pounce. "I promise I won't bite. Not unless you want me to."

I coughed while trying to take another swallow of my drink.

"No ... no ... it's just that—" I stammered.

"—you've never been with an Indian girl before ..." Manju attempted to finish my sentence. "I can assure you I have a lot of hidden talents. Like the Kama Sutra. We invented it, after all." She winked at me.

Oh lord, I was almost a goner. I turned to my left, toward the entrance of the bar, and my salvation appeared.

Prashant walked in and headed toward us.

"Hey, man," I called to him, edging myself away from Manju. A disgruntled sigh escaped her lips as if I sucked the air out of her balloon. I waved to Prashant and motioned to an empty seat on the other side of Manju. "Come join us."

When Prashant sat down, I turned to Manju. "This is Prashant. My roommate. I asked him to meet us."

"Oh. Hi." She flippantly waved her hand at him then ran a finger along my arm. "Do you want to get out of here soon?" she whispered in my ear.

His Second Chance

Ignoring Manju, I called to the bartender. "Can we get another round? My buddy here will take a Miller Lite. Get me one too, please. Manju, what do you want?"

She huffed, obviously pained that I disregarded her, and then replied, "Yeah, I'll take one, too."

"Sure thing, sweetie," the bartender replied.

A few minutes later, three pints of Miller Lite slid in front of us.

"Thanks for the beer." Prashant nodded to me. "You know what I like."

"Manju, if you want something else, tell me and I'll get it for you," I told her.

"No, I'm good," she said, taking a sip. "This is the only kind I like, too."

"Because it's light—" Prashant interrupted.

"And doesn't have a lot of calories," Manju finished his sentence.

Manju nodded toward the tattoo on Prashant's forearm. "What does your ink mean?"

"I just got it. It's an infinity symbol with a question mark," Prashant explained the unique marking. "Meaning 'Question everything.' I designed it."

"Yeah, I designed mine too," Manju replied. "But you can't see it because it's on my back. It's pretty rare to find another Indian person with a tattoo."

"So, your parents aren't aware of it?" Prashant provoked her.

"Hell no!"

His Second Chance

"Because if they were, they wouldn't be able to make you marketable to be married off!" Prashant joked.

"Don't even get me started on arranged marriages!" Manju volleyed back with an eye roll. "This isn't the 1950s, but my parents don't grasp that." She leaned toward Prashant, away from me. "They think because they had an arranged marriage that I should too." Manju scoffed. "No way. Maybe I should marry a white guy to piss them off."

"Yeah, my parents are the same way," Prashant commiserated. "My mother keeps nagging me to go to a tailor to get measured so that she can get the correct size sherwani for me."

Manju laughed out loud.

"Do you eat meat?" Manju asked Prashant.

"On any day that ends in Y," Prashant bragged. "Shhh. Don't tell my parents."

"I won't tell them as you don't tell mine that I get a burger from Hemingway's every Friday," Manju replied.

"My lips are sealed." Prashant lifted his hand to the side of his mouth and motioned as if he zipped them shut.

The butterfly resurrected.

I smiled, happy that I set Prashant and Manju's stars back in alignment.

Without drawing attention to myself, I inched my way to the other side of Prashant and let him chat with Manju for the next hour.

A green neon Rolling Rock sign on the bar wall sizzled as it burned out.

His Second Chance

Chapter 20

"Babe, can you pick up our dry cleaning after work today?" a female voice echoed from my living room. "The place left me some messages this week and I keep forgetting."

I stood in my kitchen, eyeing a Keurig coffee machine on the counter and a two-person wood and metal dining set, curious to figure out the owner of that voice. It wasn't Maggie, I was sure about that.

"Sure thing." I wandered into the hall toward the living room and the sound. I remembered being in this two-story walkup in my mid 30s, a block off of Logan Circle, in Washington, D.C. My black mountain bike rested against the exposed red brick interior wall.

What year was it?

I checked my watch: "FR12. 4.09 7:22 a.m."

Friday, December 4, 2009.

I jumped ten years. Why ten? Every other jump was less than five. Nothing made sense. I thought I had some answers, but maybe I didn't. Somebody was fucking with me and I didn't like it.

127

His Second Chance

In the living room, I came face-to-face with Rebecca. She wore a slim, navy blue skirt that accentuated her curves, a white, silk top unbuttoned above her chest, and black, killer boots that dug into my back at one time. Her wavy, chestnut hair cascaded down her back. I remembered that Rebecca and I met after grad school at a mutual friend's 30th birthday party and we dated for a few years.

"After work today, don't forget we are meeting Sam and Ellie for drinks at some new place called ChurchKey," Rebecca stated. "It's two blocks away on 14th Street, so let's come back here after work and walk over after you get the dry cleaning."

"Sounds like a plan," I told her. If I remembered correctly, Ellie was Rebecca's best friend, and Sam was Ellie's fiancé.

Rebecca stepped toward me, her heeled boots clacking on the hardwood floor, and kissed me. She shrugged into a leather jacket and grabbed her bag. "I gotta get moving or I'll miss my train," she said. "Are you getting ready for work soon?" She eyed up my attire of black sweatpants and a matching GW sweatshirt.

I glanced down at my rumpled clothes. "Um, yeah."

"Okay, see you after work. Love you." Rebecca opened the front door to the winter air, stepped onto the iron staircase, and descended to the sidewalk below.

After she left, I glanced around the first floor, trying to get my bearings. Framed pictures of Rebecca and me occupied shelves next to copies of *The Great Gatsby* and *To Kill a Mockingbird*. Another shelf housed DVDs. I ran my finger over *The Princess Bride*, all of the *Rocky* series, and *Indiana Jones*. A couple sets of our shoes sat scattered on the floor near the front door. Obviously, we lived

His Second Chance

together. Her bare hands in the pictures indicated that we weren't engaged. I exhaled that this was the same version with her as the first time around.

I wandered back into the kitchen and found my laptop on the counter next to Rebecca's grandmother's antique spoon rest.

Taking a seat at the table, I opened the laptop and tried to figure out why I was in 2009. My Gmail account popped up, beckoning a password. I typed a few characters in, hoping that the password I used in the present worked. In a few seconds, my Gmail inbox listed 40 emails and a new one from Prashant sent two hours earlier. I clicked it open.

`Dude, when are you getting a Facebook account? I've reconnected with a lot of people from CMU on it already. You need to do it. Here's the link … AGAIN.`

Chuckling to myself, knowing that Facebook was the lifeblood for most people in their 40s, I clicked the link and created an account. Immediately, Prashant's Facebook friends popped up on my screen as friend suggestions. One of them was our old dorm-mate Kevin. I clicked on Kevin's profile and sent him a friend request. Within three minutes, Kevin accepted my invitation. He must have been on his computer. Typical. I made myself a mental note to catch up with him later. I clicked on Kevin's Friends. My eyes popped when I viewed a picture of Maggie listed as his Sister. Sucking in a deep breath, I clicked "Add Friend" next to her name. My heart thumped inside my chest as I waited and waited for her response. It was amazing to me that no matter where or what I was

His Second Chance

doing at the time, if my thoughts drifted to Maggie, my entire body chemistry shifted.

Five minutes went by with no reply from Maggie. Rubbing the scar on my hand, I sighed heavily, disappointed that Maggie might not want to reconnect with me. When was the last time I talked to her? Fifteen years in her timeframe? Was that right? Maybe she forgot about me? What if she didn't want to talk to me? What if she moved on?

I spun my worries into something positive. Maybe she wasn't near her computer? Maybe she was on her way to work? Maybe she was helping her kids get ready for school? Those cute, little kids would be seven years older since the last time I encountered them in Boston.

To pass the time waiting for Maggie, I heeded Rebecca's advice from earlier. I worked at Deloitte at this time in my life. I trudged up the stairs to the bedroom and stripped off my clothes to take a shower.

Standing naked in the narrow bathroom, my mind wandered to Maggie as I turned on the water. She had always loved to dress in a way that made me want to do naughty things with her. Even snug jeans and a T-shirt made me want to run my hands all over her warm, soft skin. My heart skipped a beat whenever she wore a short skirt and leather boots. Oh, those legs could wrap around me any time they wanted.

As in direct response to my thoughts, my body reacted as any red-blooded, heterosexual male's would. I missed Maggie and so did

His Second Chance

my body. What I wouldn't do to be inside Maggie at that moment. Being between her legs was a man's paradise.

I stepped inside the steaming shower and took care of things. Imagining Maggie in front of me, her back along the cool tile, and her fingers wrapped in my hair, I wanted to kneel down and pleasure her with my mouth. Our first shower together in undergrad entered my head. Once I passed my initial nervousness back then, we found a sexy, hot rhythm and knocked the shampoo bottles to the floor in the process. What a night.

Ten minutes later, I dried off, wrapped a towel around my waist, and headed toward the bedroom. More pictures of Rebecca and me populated the nightstand. Rebecca was smart; she received her Master's from George Washington University. She could hang with me while I watched football, and plans with friends filled our weekends. I respected her and we had a good time together.

Rebecca was lovely, but how could I imagine a future with her while my mind wandered to Maggie? That wasn't fair to Rebecca. She deserved someone who put her first. She should never be someone's consolation prize.

I pulled a pair of dark jeans out of the dresser and yanked them on. Then I grabbed a Kelly green T-shirt from the drawer and threw it on. Not the work attire that Rebecca expected, but it would do.

I shuffled down the stairs, entered the kitchen, and checked my laptop again. Still no response from Maggie. My heart sank. Maybe she forgot about me? Maybe she wasn't as smitten with me as I was with her? Maybe I had imagined everything how we felt about each other?

His Second Chance

Ding.

My computer pinged with a notification, drawing me out of my spiral of discouraging thoughts. Maggie accepted my friend request! She didn't forget me after all. I clicked on her "About" menu to learn more about her life. Studied at University of Pennsylvania. No relationship status to show. But that didn't mean she wasn't in one. I assumed she was still married to that giant frat guy I saw her with in Boston. What was his name again? Maverick. No, Brett. That's right. Brett. Maggie's work and education section stated, "Works at Baltimore Museum of Art." Baltimore? That's only an hour away. How did she end up in Baltimore? When did she leave Boston? I wanted to know all about her life that I missed.

Immediately, I opened a new message box and typed: `Hi Maggie - Thanks for connecting with me. What have you been up to? I hope to hear from you soon. Ryan`

Trying hard not to sound needy and desperate, I hit "Send" hoping that she didn't discover my façade.

I closed my laptop and headed back to the living room, attempting to distract myself with bad, daytime TV until Maggie replied.

A couple of hours later, I awoke with a start to the sound of a random, kids TV show theme song. I patted myself and exhaled, realizing I was still in the green shirt and jeans. Still in 2009 in D.C.

I stood from the couch and entered the kitchen again. Keeping my laptop in a separate room gave me a physical barrier to prevent me from checking it every 15 seconds waiting for Maggie to respond.

When I flipped it open, I puffed out a sigh of relief when I read a message from her: Hi Ryan! So good to hear from you! It's been forever. What have I been up to?? Where should I start?? Too bad you don't live nearby, otherwise we could meet for coffee sometime soon and I could fill you in with what's been happening in my life. Lots to tell.

Of course, Maggie didn't know that I was only an hour away from her now. Stupid me never set up my Facebook profile stating where I lived. I could easily get to Baltimore and meet her for lunch.

I replied: In fact, I do live nearby. Somewhat. I'm in D.C. Let me know when you are free and I'll be there.

A few seconds later, Maggie wrote: How about tomorrow?

Tomorrow? The next day was Saturday, so obviously, I didn't have to be at work, but how would I explain to Rebecca that I wanted to head to Baltimore. I needed to come up with a plan.

Yes, tomorrow can work, I wrote in anticipation of deception. Give me a time and place. I hated lying to anyone, especially Rebecca, but I was not about to pass up an opportunity to spend time with Maggie. Even after all these years. God, I missed her.

Chapter 21

A few hours later, Rebecca came home carrying an armful of clothes wrapped in plastic. "You're off the hook," she told me. "I ended up meeting a client near the dry cleaners this afternoon so I picked them up myself. I hope you didn't go over there."

I stood from the couch, grabbed the freshly cleaned clothes from Rebecca, and kissed her on the cheek. "Thanks, babe. I'll take these upstairs."

After I hung the clothes up in our closet and returned downstairs, I found Rebecca in the kitchen.

"My mom called me today," she said. "She will be in Richmond tomorrow for the weekend and she wants to spend time with me."

"Oh great!"

Rebecca rolled her eyes at me and pursed her lips. "She's only coming into town because she wants something. You know that's her M.O."

His Second Chance

"Oh. Right." Mimicking her facial features, I couldn't remember what Rebecca's mother was like, so I kept my response short and vague.

"Don't worry. You're off the hook," Rebecca stated. "I'll go visit her by myself and see what she wants. It might be most of the weekend, though, so I'm sure you can find something to do."

"I'll be fine," I told her. I tried to hide my excitement that I didn't need to come up with a lie to tell Rebecca in order to go see Maggie. Rebecca opened the window of opportunity for me and the wind blew in with gusto. "Don't worry about me. I'll be okay by myself."

"Are you sure?" Rebecca must have felt bad for leaving me all weekend. "Maybe talk to Sam tonight and find out what he's doing? Maybe the Caps are in town?"

"Yeah, I'm sure."

I followed Rebecca up the stairs to the second floor, my hand grazing her ass. Even if she wasn't the love of my life, I still found her hot.

"We don't have time for that," Rebecca cooed. "We have to meet Sam and Ellie in 15 minutes."

"I only need five."

* * * *

Twenty minutes later, Rebecca and I hustled down 14th Street and stopped in front of an old, brown, two-story building that might have been a former fire department. A large, glass-paneled garage door took up most of the first-floor frontage, while oversized windows offered a panoramic view to the second story. A brown and yellow vertical sign up the right side of the building said CHURCHKEY. Mounds of shoveled snow piled up on both sides of the building, giving it a guarded vibe.

We stomped the snow off our shoes, I opened the door to the entrance, and held it open for Rebecca to go in front of me. Patrons munching on pub food and drinking beer at brown and orange tables filled the first floor. Lively conversations carried throughout the long and narrow room. Gold, sconce lanterns provided intimate ambiance along the perimeter walls.

"Ellie called and said they are upstairs." Rebecca motioned toward the mahogany staircase that led to the second floor.

At the top of the stairs, more patrons filled booths along the velvet padded wall. Round wooden chandeliers hung from the ceiling. Half a dozen TVs displayed football, hockey, and basketball games in between overhead racks of Jameson and Glenfiddich—a sports lover's paradise. Sam and Ellie sat at the far end of the bar, saving two empty stools for us.

Sam waved us over. He wore a chocolate-colored sweater that matched his dark skin and a plaid grey and red scarf wrapped around his neck. Ellie was dressed in an ivory turtleneck sweater that contrasted her dark curly hair and skin. They could have been models for *Essence*.

"Sorry we're late," Rebecca told them as we exchanged hello kisses and hugs. "We had to ... uh ... do something."

Sam chuckled and winked at me.

His Second Chance

"What do you want to drink?" I asked Rebecca. Several dozen taps lined the back wall of the bar area.

"Surprise me," she replied. "You know what I like."

I turned from my friends and caught the attention of the bartender. Apprehension rushed through me as I tried to guess what Rebecca would like on a menu I had never seen before. The long row of drafts in front of me made my head spin. This time-traveling shit was messing with me, for sure.

"Have you been here before?" the hipster, bearded bartender asked me.

"No, first time."

"Okay, then let me help you," he said while resting his palms on the shiny counter between us. "What do you like?"

"Something hoppy," I told him.

"I have the perfect thing for you," he replied with a pointed finger. "Thin Man. It's a double IPA out of New York."

"Give me two," I told him.

After I exchanged my credit card for the two snifters of beer, I turned back to Rebecca, Sam, and Ellie who were deep in conversation. I handed one of the beers to Rebecca.

"Here you go, babe," I told her.

After two more glasses of Thin Man, the excessive booze made me loopy. Usually, three beers didn't affect me this fast. What was going on? Then I narrowed my eyes at the alcohol percentage on the beer list on the wall: Thin Man 8%. Holy shit. No wonder I was lightheaded after only three. Good thing we walked over.

His Second Chance

I caught Rebecca's attention in the midst of listening to Ellie talk about her upcoming wedding with Sam. "I'm gonna order a Monster Energy Drink to help counterbalance the beer, do you want one?"

"No, you can't," she said, grasping my forearm. "Remember, the doctor told you to limit your caffeine."

Even though I didn't recall the doctor's orders, I had to believe that Rebecca was correct. She had a good heart. She was an admirable girlfriend, watching out for my health. I couldn't have asked for anything better, except for maybe Maggie. Tomorrow would be here soon enough. Then I'd see Maggie again. I couldn't wait to see her. My heart jumped inside my chest.

I turned to the bartender and ordered a seltzer with a lime twist instead.

HIS SECOND CHANCE

Chapter 22

The next morning, I awoke in bed with Rebecca sleeping beside me. I still couldn't figure out why some nights I jumped to another time and sometimes I didn't. I snuggled Rebecca in my arms and she woke up in the process.

"What time is it?" she asked with a drowsy tone.

"Almost nine," I told her.

"Crap!" She leapt out of bed, knocking the covers to the floor, and stood half-naked in front of me wearing panties and a tank top. "I gotta go! I told my mother I'd meet her at noon and it's a two-hour drive to Richmond." She bolted toward the bathroom.

"Anything you want me to do?" I called after her.

"Get me some coffee," she yelled from the sink. "And please find my weekend bag."

* * * *

HIS SECOND CHANCE

After Rebecca left to see her mother, I opened my laptop and logged into Facebook as I settled into the couch. The Saturday morning news on TV talked about upcoming holiday festivals, driving carefully on ice, and a couple of dumbasses who were arrested for snowboarding at the Thomas Jefferson Memorial.

A message from Maggie popped up on my screen: `Ryan, want to meet me for lunch at noon at the Thames Street Oyster House in Fells Point?`

I immediately confirmed lunch with Maggie and headed upstairs to get ready. I needed to be out the door by 10:30 to get to Baltimore and park. After I took a quick shower, I shaved and splashed on some cologne. What would I wear? I couldn't appear like I tried too hard, even though I was. Standing at the closet, I grabbed a blue and white, small, checkered button-down shirt and put it on. I pulled on some dark jeans and stepped into a pair of loafers. My heart thumped out of my chest, excited that I would be with Maggie.

At 11:55, I walked up to the Thames Street Oyster House, a sky-blue building nestled between an old pub and the Fells Point Visitor Center. To my good fortune, I found parking on the grey cobblestone road right in front of the restaurant. Across the street, boats festooned with multi-colored lights filled the marina. The chilly December air created a mystical fog along the water. Then I noticed a sign for the annual Fells Point Christmas Boat Parade. A set of holiday string lights blinked above me.

His Second Chance

Inside the oyster house, I maneuvered my way around the filled tables at the front of the restaurant and approached the hostess at a formerly-used black music stand.

"Hi, I'm meeting someone for lunch," I explained. "A blonde woman. I don't know if she's already here."

The hostess replied, "I just seated her. She's upstairs. Please follow me."

On the second floor, Maggie sat alone at a table along the red brick wall of the original tavern. Wow, she looked good. Even after all these years. She still had the face of a twenty-five-year-old, even though she was in her late thirties. Her blonde hair fell into waves on her shoulders and her face didn't show signs of any wrinkles.

Maggie wore a red sweater that dipped down into a V above her chest. Libidinous thoughts of kissing what lay beneath that sweater crossed my mind. She was the only woman who'd ever turned me on simply by wearing something. Maggie waved me over to join her. A Christmas wreath hung on the wall next to her.

She stood from her chair and I hugged and kissed her on the cheek. "You are gorgeous. Like fine wine, you are even better with age," I told her as I took a seat on her left side.

"Thank you." She blushed, matching her sweater. I stared at her, taking in her beauty. I could get lost in those green eyes. Her luscious lips brought me back to a time where I spent hours kissing them. I wanted to kiss them again.

A female server wearing a black T-shirt with "Thames Street Oyster House" on the left breast pocket appeared at our table, interrupting my lustful thoughts.

His Second Chance

"Hi, my name is Catherine," she spoke. "Can I start you off with some drinks?"

"I'm ready to order if you are," Maggie said to me.

"You're not gonna want the Lobster Polenta." I nodded to Maggie as I quickly perused the menu. "It has mushrooms in it and I know you don't like them."

She gasped and smiled at me. "Wow! I can't believe you remembered."

"I remember almost everything about you," I told her. "It doesn't matter how long we haven't seen each other."

After Maggie and I gave Catherine our order, I rested my left hand on the table near her right one. What I wouldn't do to take that hand in mine. But she was married and I refused to put her in a compromising position. My urges took a distant second to her happiness.

"You look great," she said. "I love this shirt on you."

"Thank you." The few extra moments in my closet that morning paid off. "But how've you been? What's been happening in your life?"

Maggie puffed out a humorous sigh. "How long do you have?"

All my life, I wanted to tell her. Instead, I beamed at her and said, "I have all day."

"Where do I even start?" Maggie grabbed her water glass with her left hand and downed a gulp. Her ring finger was bare! Trying hard to contain my excitement, I took a swig of my own water to hide my wide smile.

"Start at the beginning," I directed.

His Second Chance

"Well," Maggie began, "I was married to this guy, Brett. Things were fantastic in the onset. He'd dote on me, made me breakfast, send me sweet emails. Things like that. We'd go on vacation to St. Lucia every other year. He constantly held my hand and told me how much he loved me. We lived in a nice house in Boston, in the North End."

I remembered that guy. He rushed after her with coffee in his hand in Boston and then kissed her. I hated him. But since Maggie didn't take notice of me then, I had to pretend to her now that I didn't know about him.

She continued, "We have two great kids together. Madelyn and Thomas." Maggie swallowed another gulp of water. Clearly, the story did not end well since she talked about him in past tense. I wanted to take her in my arms and hold her tight. If that guy hurt her, I would kill him.

"But then one day, about a year ago, I picked up the mail," she explained. "And guess what was delivered to me?"

"I ... I ... have no idea." Even though her story intrigued me, I couldn't even guess.

"Several photos of Brett kissing another woman!" Maggie shrieked. "Half-naked! In our bedroom!"

"No way!"

"Yes way," she answered, quieter. "I was in shock. I even think I threw up. When I confronted him about it, he denied it at first. But then he confessed, saying the affair had been going on for years. Years!" Maggie scoffed and shook her head in disgust. "Everything he did for me and to me was a lie. I was such a fool to think he cared

His Second Chance

about me. I still can't believe he did that to me. I never found out who sent me those pictures, though."

My insides twisted, realizing that what I witnessed in Boston was a sham, but the other part of me sympathized with Maggie. My heart ached for her. She didn't deserve to be treated like that. Why on Earth would anyone cheat on such an amazing woman like her?

"So, I filed for divorce," Maggie continued. "Brett didn't fight it because he knew he was wrong. But I couldn't stay in Boston anymore. Too many bad memories. I packed the kids up and moved to Baltimore. I landed an awesome job at the Museum of Art. My kids don't visit their dad as often as they should though. Brett keeps saying he'll move closer to spend time with them on a regular basis, but it hasn't happened yet, so I'm not holding my breath." Maggie let out a disgruntled groan. "He's too busy with his skanky whore. Oops, did I say that out loud?"

I laughed lightly at Maggie's joke.

"So, for the first time in a long time, I'm single," Maggie stated, with a half-smile.

"Have you gone on a date with anyone since?" I asked.

"Hell no," Maggie scoffed. "I need to get my own shit together first." She clamped a hand over her mouth. "Sorry I'm cursing so much. I was pissed for a long time and I'm finally starting to feel like myself again."

"It's okay," I reassured her. "You're entitled. He's an idiot."

Maggie laughed out loud.

For the next hour, Maggie and I chatted nonstop while dining on an Old Bay Shrimp Salad Roll and a Chesapeake Blue Catfish

His Second Chance

sandwich. As we shared strawberry cobbler for dessert, I found myself staring at Maggie. She was still so beautiful and made me feel warm inside.

We had a couple of drinks with our lunch. Sparkling conversation carried the afternoon as we caught up on our lives. It had been many years since we had last spoken in person. I missed her and it showed, by how engrossed I was in every little detail of her life that she filled me in on. I stared at her soft lips, her bright eyes, and her pink cheeks while she talked. When she listened to me, she would interject with this incredibly sexy "Mmm-hmm" that made me tremble hearing it right up against my ear.

Catching my ogle, Maggie said, "What? Do I have something on my face?"

"No ... no ..." I stammered, embarrassed that she caught me. "You just ... look ... stunning ... I'm sorry if I'm being too bold." Again, I couldn't bring myself to tell her my feelings for her. Even given a second chance to make things right, I lacked the nerve to say anything because we had been away from each other for so long. I wanted to shout from the rooftops how much I loved her. But I didn't want to pressure her into anything she wasn't ready for. Not after her harrowing divorce. I refused to be that guy.

After I paid the bill, Maggie and I lingered outside the front of the restaurant on the sidewalk as locals passed us on the narrow throughway. How could I spend more time with Maggie without sounding too eager? She jingled keys in her hand, but made no attempt to step away from me. Was that a sign?

"Where are you going now? Heading back home?" she asked.

His Second Chance

"I don't have any plans," I replied. I hadn't considered Rebecca in the past hour, but I had some time on my hands. Nor did I want to leave Maggie. "Don't you have to get back to your kids?"

"No," she answered. "They are with their dad for the weekend. He actually came to visit them this weekend and they are staying at his hotel. So ... if you're up for it ..." Maggie rattled her keys rapidly, in a nervous way. "Would you like to come with me to the aquarium? I like to go there and clear my head. It's only about a mile walk from here." She motioned to the bare walkway in front of us. "The sidewalks are paved so it should be an easy walk."

Would I! Any additional time spent with Maggie was like getting extra cheese on my pizza for free. I loved her endearing qualities. She made me believe I was the only man in the world. Just for her.

I took a step closer to her and linked her right elbow in my left. "I'd love to. Let's go."

She chuckled at my feeble attempt at flirting with her and we headed west down the sidewalk toward the aquarium. She pressed her shoulder against mine as we walked. It was a cold winter afternoon, but where she touched me, it felt like a warm spring day.

His Second Chance

Chapter 23

A half hour later, after passing 18th-century maritime buildings blanketed in holiday decorations on our right on East Pratt Street and the Patapsco River on our left, we arrived at the National Aquarium. Inner Harbor snoozed in the winter afternoon, taking a break from massive summer crowds. The enormous glass aquarium building gleaned in the cool temperatures, reflecting bare trees from the plaza and other quiet buildings onto its sides.

Maggie and I spent the next three hours wandering the interior halls of the aquarium gazing at harmonious jellyfish, stealthy sharks, and prismatic fish. I wanted to hold her hand, but was still unsure of how she would react, so I curbed myself. Occasionally, she'd graze my arm with her fingers as we talked about the mysterious animals lurking on the top floor's tropical rainforest. We also chatted about what we both accomplished in our lives and the dreams we still had.

"Is there anything in your life you regret?" I asked Maggie, as I pushed a rogue strand of blonde hair out of her face.

His Second Chance

"I can't say I regret marrying Brett." She offered a weak smile. "Because then I wouldn't have Madelyn and Thomas. They are great kids." She pondered my broad question for a few more seconds. "But no, I can't say I've regretted anything. I could die tomorrow and be content. What about you? Anything you regret?"

The answer stood right in front of me. But I couldn't tell her. Not yet. Not until I landed safely back in the present—with her. Maggie was my past, present, and future. I still wasn't sure how I would make it happen, but I couldn't let her slip away again.

"I have everything I've ever wanted," I told her. The answer was true, but still vague enough that she wouldn't ask any secondary questions.

Suddenly, my phone buzzed, interrupting us. I pulled it out of my pocket and viewed the name on the screen. Rebecca. Damn.

"I'm so sorry," I told Maggie. "I have to take this." In the few seconds I took stepping away from Maggie to a quiet corner of the aquarium, I calmed myself down and mentally separated the two women in my life.

"Hi, Bec," I quietly said into the phone. "How's the visit with your mom?"

"Not as terrible as I expected," she replied. "She wanted to see me for the weekend before she got on the road again. You know how she is. Always traveling."

"That's good," I mumbled. As Rebecca's next words fluttered into my ear, I gazed over at Maggie who was intently investigating a scarlet ibis that unsuccessfully tried to go incognito amongst the lush green foliage. I didn't grasp a word Rebecca spoke.

His Second Chance

"Did you hear what I said?" Rebecca raised her tone, trying to catch my attention.

"Uh, no ... sorry, babe ..." I stuttered, still studying Maggie.

"I said I won't be home until tomorrow night," Rebecca replied.

"That's fine." I didn't want to tell her that I was thankful for the extra time away from her. Guilt seeped into my mind but I brushed it away. "I'll see you then. Bye, babe."

After I hung up with Rebecca, I sauntered through the crowd of tourists back over to Maggie.

"Is everything okay?"

"Yeah, all good," I told her. Then I guided Maggie through the rest of the rainforest exhibit. I wasn't ready to tell her about Rebecca. Not yet.

* * * *

At 5:00, Maggie and I exited the aquarium as the December sun set along Inner Harbor sending pink and orange streams across the sky. She shuddered in the winter wind.

"I'll keep you warm." I wrapped my arm around her shoulder and pulled her close to me as we walked out of the plaza back toward Fells Point. Lights from boats in the Christmas Boat Parade twinkled in the water, giving us a personal display.

"Should we get a cab? It's a good mile back to your car." Maggie gazed up at me with green, doe-like eyes. I could get lost in them.

His Second Chance

"Nah, I like strolling with you," I replied. "But where did you park?"

"I didn't," Maggie quipped. "I live a couple of blocks away from the Oyster House. I walked over."

Stopping myself from jumping up and down with excitement, I squeezed Maggie into me. Her house was empty and we had spent a glorious afternoon together. How I wished to do so many naughty things to her. But I hesitated because of what she said earlier. I would never put her in an uncomfortable situation by pressuring her to do something that she wasn't ready for.

We made a right on President Street, passing a building with a giant underwater sea mural. Downtown skyscrapers sparkled in the evening sun. I wasn't familiar with Baltimore, so I let Maggie take the lead as we made a left onto Fleet Street.

"Are we taking a shortcut back to Thames Street?" I asked Maggie. The buildings around us didn't look familiar to me.

"No," she replied, gazing up at me. "I thought we'd stop at my place for a glass of wine. I think I can whip up something to eat for dinner if you want. Are you hungry?"

"Yes. I'm all in." I beamed at her.

Ten minutes later, we approached a turn-of-the-century, blue-sided, two-story house nestled between a couple of red brick homes. Red and white shutters accented the cute home. Two small, decorated Christmas trees flanked the glass-paneled front door. Adorable, like Maggie. She pulled a key out of her pocket and unlocked the door.

His Second Chance

"Welcome to my humble abode," she told me as we stepped into her living room. "It's not much, but it's mine." A brown leather couch huddled in the corner next to a lofty Christmas tree that gleamed with white lights and bright-colored ornaments. A few presents wrapped in gold paper and white bows settled under the tree. The scent of cinnamon lingered in the air.

"It's cute," I told her. I followed her into the modern kitchen with exposed brick walls. She reached into an overhead wine rack above one of the countertops.

"Red or white?" Maggie asked me.

"Red," I answered.

Maggie found a bottle of Malbec and poured us each a glass of wine. I clinked her glass with mine. "Thank you for having me over."

"Of course," she replied. She glanced at me a second longer as if she reflected on something about me, then took a sip. What was she thinking about? "Are you hungry now? I have some shrimp and pasta I could whip up. Wanna help?"

"Sure, that'd be great," I told her. With direction, I assisted Maggie gathering pots and pans out of her cabinets as we prepared dinner together. Everything seemed effortless with her. Usually I didn't like to make meals for only myself, but she made it easy by being together. We drank wine as we talked and cooked, so I refilled our glasses.

When Maggie was in my way in the tight kitchen, I placed my hands on her waist, still keeping a few inches between us, and moved her in another direction. I so wanted to bend her backwards over the

His Second Chance

countertop and have my way with her, but I wasn't sure how she would react to my assertive move. I would always defer to her wishes. After her atrocious marriage, she deserved the best.

With plates of shrimp and pasta and a side salad, we settled in at her kitchen table. A sparkly, vintage chandelier suspended from the ceiling above us.

"I love this table." She ran a palm over the mahogany surface. "My brother found it at a yard sale and thought it was perfect for me after my divorce." My mind wandered to our naked bodies doing naughty things on top of that table. Kissing her electrified me, fueling my body with adrenaline.

"It's nice," I told her. "Kevin has good taste." And a hot sister, I wanted to add.

I filled our wine glasses again, emptying the bottle.

"Whatever happened between us, Ryan?" Maggie posed the bold question. Maybe the added wine gave her some liquid courage. "Why did we never get together?"

I blew out a nervous sigh. "It was my fault," I told her. "You were always so wonderful and lovely. I recall our first date so vividly."

"Tell me what you remember." Maggie leaned toward me, exposing the deep cleavage of her red, V-neck sweater. "I mean, I know what I recall, but tell me what *you* remember."

I smiled broadly at her. That day was one of my favorites. "We went to a CMU football game that afternoon, but I don't remember if we stayed the whole game. It was September, so it was too warm to huddle under a blanket."

His Second Chance

"Yes, I remember," Maggie added, grazing my arm with hers. "I kept the game ticket as a memento for a long time after that."

I continued, "Then we attempted to play pool at the union building, but all of the tables were full, so I borrowed a frisbee from one of my dorm-mates and we played on the quad. It was so much fun."

"I was terrible," Maggie lamented. "I remember you running all over the field after my bad throws."

"But it was fun," I said. "I was with a cute girl—the envy of all my geeky friends—and I didn't mind."

She offered me a sheepish grin.

"Then I remember taking you to dinner at a pub in Shadyside a few blocks away where we ate burgers and fries," I reminisced. "We stayed there for a couple hours, laughing and talking. You were so easy to talk to, even on our first date. Still are. You're good at getting me to disclose things. I tend to keep things inside."

"It's a blessing and a curse," Maggie chuckled at her own joke. "Sometimes it's nice to have people open up, but other times I don't care what someone had for dinner the previous day or how much laundry they did. Does that make me a heartless bitch?"

I laughed with her and continued my memory. "Then, after dinner, I remember it was dark and we walked around the CMU campus and it started to rain. I grabbed your hand as we darted in and out of the alcoves of the buildings trying not to get wet. Then we stopped at the Fine Arts building—"

His Second Chance

"And you kissed me," Maggie finished my sentence, taking another swig of wine. "Our first kiss. We stood in a secluded spot and made out."

"It was sweet and intimate," I replied. That memory burned in my brain after all this time. I couldn't remember kissing someone like that on a previous first date.

After two hours of chatting and finishing another bottle of wine, Maggie raised a hand to her forehead and briefly closed her eyes.

"You okay?" I asked.

"I think I've had too much to drink," she said, opening her eyes. "This wine is getting to me."

"Good thing we don't have to drive," I joked.

"But you need to go home, don't you?" she asked in more of a statement than a question.

"No," I told her, "I'm staying here with you."

Maggie glared at me, thinking the worst.

"No, I mean I'll sleep on your couch," I corrected myself. "I need to make sure you're okay. Plus, I shouldn't be driving anyway."

"Okay." Maggie bobbed her head up and down. The wine had a cute affect on her.

"I'll help you get ready for bed, then I'll find myself a blanket and pillow," I told her. "Don't worry, I won't peek."

Maggie giggled at my joke. Wow, she was so cute.

We stood from the table. I cleared our dishes and put them in the dishwasher.

His Second Chance

Fifteen minutes later, Maggie was fast asleep curled up in her bed. I smiled to myself, happy that she was safe and sound. I pillaged her linen closet, found a blanket and an extra pillow, and settled on her couch for the night.

I hoped I didn't jump because I wanted to spend time with Maggie in the morning. She warmed my heart. Even though we had been away from each other for fifteen years in her lifespan, it only seemed like yesterday.

HIS SECOND CHANCE

Chapter 24

The next morning, Maggie greeted me on the edge of her couch with two cups of coffee, offering me one. "I am so sorry about last night," she stated. "I haven't had that much to drink in a long time. I see you found yourself a blanket and pillow. Sorry you had to sleep in your clothes."

"It's okay. I had a great time with you, so that made up for it," I told her, taking a sip of the hot arabica mixture. Thank god I didn't jump.

"Did I say anything stupid?" she asked me. Maggie wore a light blue tank top and sleep shorts, not the sweater and pants I left her in last night. Wow, she looked cute.

"No," I chuckled. "You were fine." More than fine. With my left hand, I set my cup of coffee on the table next to the couch.

"But now I'm completely sober," she deadpanned, placing her mug next to mine. She pulled something red and lacy out of her shorts pocket. A matching bra and panty set. "I wore these all day yesterday. You could have seen them on me."

156

His Second Chance

Holy hell. Blood rushed through me, realizing exactly what she meant. My heart pounded full throttle inside my chest. After all this time, she wanted me as much as I wanted her.

"Put them back on," I instructed her. I could say it was her fault for showing me her lingerie, but my mind could be a nasty place with the blame squarely on me.

Without a word, Maggie stepped away from me to the far side of the living room, with her back to me. Silently, I studied her as she lowered her sleep shorts, but her tank top covered most of her bare ass. What I wouldn't do to pull that ass into me. She slipped the red panties up her legs and then removed her tank top, exposing her bare back. Her luscious bare back that curved into her beautiful hips. She slipped the red bra on, then turned around and walked toward me wearing the matching set.

Instantly, my cock swelled to attention beneath my jeans. She owned me. She took the breath out of me without even trying. Maggie was a work of art.

Maggie slowly approached the couch and, as soon as she was within arm's length, I yanked her on top of me, kissing her mouth, her neck, her face. My hands explored every part of her body, grasping every inch that I could reach.

While kissing me, Maggie reached for my belt buckle and unhooked it. Then she unbuttoned my jeans and unzipped them. She slid a warm hand down my pants, edging her fingers along my hip bone. I groaned in response.

"You like my hand there?" she whispered in my ear.

"Yes," was all I could utter.

His Second Chance

My clothing suffocated me under her spell. I grabbed the waistband of my jeans and pushed them down. Maggie giggled in response and placed her hand on mine and helped me take my pants off my legs, leaving me in my boxers. My hard cock rose upward, expanding the space in my drawers.

Maggie grasped my shirt in her hands and pulled it upward, over my head, not bothering to unbutton it. Her skin against mine brought me to another place, heating every neuron inside me.

Kissing my ear, Maggie softly mmm'd. "I love how you taste," she sighed as she licked the side of my neck. She continued with her sexy commentary, "I want to taste more of you."

With that, she began kissing and licking a trail from my shoulder down to my chest. My body was on fire. My cock pressed itself so hard against my boxer briefs that I thought it would tear the fabric.

With a deft flick of her wrist, Maggie pulled my underwear down to reveal my tumid shaft. My body trembled with desire. "Are you cold, baby?" she cooed. "Let's get you hot."

As her soft, sexy mouth encircled my cock, I ached. She made me harder than I ever knew I could get. I wanted to please her so much, but I was pinned.

Maggie's hot mouth slid slowly up and down my shaft as she made a sexy "Mmmm" noise on it. I didn't want to release so quickly—she felt so damn good! I reached down and grabbed her smooth legs, pulling her upside down on top of me. With my hot mouth on her sexy panties, I made an "Mmm" sound of my own against her salacious paradise and pulled her panties to the side so I could taste her wonderful pussy.

With that, Maggie shifted her body and straddled me to regain control of the situation. The blood returned to my solid cock. To further fortify her command and control, Maggie slid her hot, wet pussy back and forth over my cock, moaning softly as it pulsed against her.

"Don't move, Ryan, I'm almost there," she begged as her pussy ground harder against my thick shaft. "Stay there ... please." I tried to ignore her plea, but damn if she wasn't so hot when she talked to me like that. I loved taking orders from her ... especially when I witnessed the intoxicating results.

As she came, her whole body shuddered on top of me and it made me so hot. She collapsed onto my chest and slid her body down my legs. As her breasts reached my cock, it stretched out to meet them and she smiled widely at me.

Rubbing her soft, sexy cleavage on my cock made me groan loud enough for the neighbors to hear. She locked eyes with me for the millisecond it took to recognize lust and then lowered her chin to draw the head of my cock into her mouth again.

Oh my god she felt so good ... like hot, wet silk wrapped around me. Soft and tight and vibrating with her sexy moans. As her mouth slid slowly up and down my shaft, I could feel more and more of it going in with each thrust. "Baby, you're going to make me cum," I half-protested.

"I'm counting on it," was the last thing she said before taking my tight balls in her warm hand and massaging them. Two or three more sexy wet thrusts of her mouth was all it took to make my entire body tighten as I exploded so hard. She kept the head of my cock in her lips tightly as she swirled her tongue around my tip. I exploded for what seemed like an entire minute.

"Mmmm that's how you make me feel, baby," she said with a satisfied smile.

Exhausted, I curled Maggie next to me on the couch. Her heart beat frantically beneath my embrace. I traced a finger along her shoulder and neck.

"Damn, if your skin isn't the best-feeling skin I've ever touched," I told her. "It's like you bathe in milk or something."

She giggled. "I'll let you in on a little secret. It's all smoke and mirrors," she confessed. "I have terribly dry skin. Like Mojave Desert dry. I lather shea butter on it every day."

"Well, you could've fooled me," I admitted. I took her face in my hands and directed it toward mine to kiss it. "What do you have going on for the rest of the day?"

"Not much," she said. "My kids aren't coming back until tonight. You?"

"I want to stay right here with you," I admitted. I never wanted to leave Maggie again.

"But don't you have to go back home eventually?" she asked me. "Don't you have fish to feed or mail to pick up or your job tomorrow?"

Oh my god. Home. And Rebecca. She completely slipped my mind. What did I do? I was never one to cheat, but Maggie made me toss all of those moral rules out the window. She was my kryptonite.

His Second Chance

I had to end things with Rebecca. She deserved someone who loved her, and didn't treat her like Ms. Right Now.

"Um, yeah," I stuttered, still trying to figure out what I needed to do with Rebecca. I couldn't tell Maggie about her either; she was too virtuous to be privy to my infidelity. "I have to head home and take care of a few things." I kissed Maggie again, then pushed her upward off of me. "But I want to come back and see you." As she twisted her naked body to face me, I kissed her again. "I want to be with you and make up for all the lost time I put you through."

"You would?" She beamed at me with a crimson glow in her cheeks. Her green eyes hypnotized me. So cute. "I want to be with you, too."

"Good," I told her. "Give me a few days to take care of things back home and I can come back next weekend. I'll find a place to live and move here to be with you." Hopefully, I didn't jump to another time before then. "If you'll have me." I would love her until the day I die.

"Yes, I'll have you," Maggie replied. "I'm ready to do this again. I know we haven't been around each other in years, but I feel like this is the right thing for me. I love being with you. And the amazing sex is a bonus." She winked.

Holding Maggie into me, I gulped in a pocket of air knowing that I would break Rebecca's heart.

Chapter 25

A few hours later, like a caged animal, I paced the townhouse that I shared with Rebecca and rubbed the scar on my right hand until it became raw. What would I say to her? I couldn't tell her the truth about how I loved Maggie and that Rebecca was my consolation prize all this time. She would never forgive me. Hell, she might throw something at me. I couldn't gather up all of the glass picture frames or ceramic knick knacks in preparation of her wrath. She would notice as soon as she walked in the door that they were missing. Rebecca was too smart for that.

I dragged myself into the kitchen and looted through our cabinets searching for some liquid courage. A half-empty bottle of Jack Daniels caught my eye. Grabbing a clean glass out of the bordering cabinet, I filled the tumbler three fingers high and swallowed it down. Hopefully the spirits would calm my nerves. I didn't envy what Rebecca was about to go through. She deserved someone better than me.

A jingle at the front door caught my attention.

His Second Chance

"Ryan, I'm home!" Rebecca called out from the living room.

"I'm in the kitchen," I yelled to her as I set the empty glass on the counter. I stroked my scar again, trying to alleviate my anxieties.

"My mother wasn't as bad as she has been," Rebecca stated as she threw her bag down on the kitchen table. "We talked for a while. Which was why I didn't call you last night or this morning."

Guilt seeped into me because I hadn't noticed. I was too busy with Maggie.

"She's heading to Florida after New Years and asked me if we wanted to meet her there," Rebecca continued.

"Oh," was all I could utter.

"What? You don't want to go?" Rebecca glared at me, hands on her hips, waiting on an answer.

A nervous pit formed in my stomach as my heart raced. My hands instantly started to sweat. I had to tell Rebecca that I needed to break up with her. It was now or never.

"No, I don't," I began.

"Why n—"

I cut Rebecca off before she could continue and sucked in a deep breath. "Because ... I don't think we should do this anymore."

"This? This what?" Rebecca took a step toward me. Her focus darted around the kitchen. A kitchen full of our stuff. "Are you ... Are you breaking up with me?" Her eyes narrowed at me, the crease between her brows formed a deep V.

"Yes," I whispered.

The features in her face shifted from confused to utter disbelief. She blinked a few times before speaking again. A single tear trickled down her cheek. "We've been together five years! I didn't even mind that we weren't married. I told my mom yesterday that everything was going great between us. I can't believe this." She stared away from me, gazing out the doorway.

"I'm so sorry," I stated.

"How long have you felt this way?" Rebecca begged the question, backing away from me.

"A little while now," I replied. I couldn't give her a definitive answer because of my time traveling.

"Why didn't you tell me sooner?" Rebecca shot back. "I can't believe I've wasted five years with you! You let my emotions develop unfairly. I believed we would eventually get married. You completely wasted my time. You're such an ass."

"I'm so sorry," I repeated. I took a step toward Rebecca, trying to comfort her. "But you should be with someone who wants to be with you. To marry you."

"Because you *don't*?" Rebecca volleyed.

"I ... uh ..." I reached for her hand, but she quickly slipped her wrist out of my grip.

"Don't touch me," she hissed. Rebecca's eyes burned into me like daggers. "Tell me the truth why you're ending things. Is there someone else?"

Rebecca couldn't know about Maggie. I didn't have all the answers myself. Rebecca had no idea about my time traveling. Her ignorance was for the best.

"No," I lied. "I swear."

His Second Chance

"Then why are you breaking up with me?" she pleaded. "Did I do something?"

"You didn't do anything," I told her. "You've been perfect."

"Don't patronize me," Rebecca snarled. "I hate that."

I sucked in another breath and quickly thought of what I could tell her without insulting her intelligence.

"You're not—" I began "—The One."

Rebecca's mouth fell open into an O as if I said something blasphemous.

"Wow. Just wow." Rebecca scoffed at me as she tried to slide past me without touching me. She considered me a human form of horse shit.

"I'll move out," I offered. "You can have the townhouse."

"You're damn right you are!" she growled. "I want you out tonight." Her eyes focused downward and then around the room, on anything but me.

"Yes, of course," I couldn't ease Rebecca's pain, but nothing could alleviate my blindsiding her.

Wiping a tear from my cheek, I stepped out of the kitchen, leaving Rebecca alone. She would find someone who wanted to be with her as much as she wanted to be with him. I knew it. She was a catch. Just not the one for me.

Rebecca didn't realize it now, but I saved her the pain of waiting to see if I would ever propose to her. She would find the right guy, marry him, and have two kids. I was sorry that I wasted her time. When she and I first got together in my original life timeline, I wasn't sure where our relationship would head. We were comfortable then, but I made no effort to officially commit to her. She needed that commitment. And a guy who truly loved her. I wished her nothing but the best.

HIS SECOND CHANCE

Chapter 26

By 6:00, everything important to me filled a few suitcases and lay in the trunk of my car. I drove a 2008 red Mazda Miata. With the top pulled up, I swerved in and out of traffic along I-195 heading north to Baltimore. For the first time in a long time, I was in control of where I was headed, but had no idea where to go.

I couldn't go to Maggie's. Not yet. She needed to believe that I found a place to stay, instead of taking residence at her house. I didn't want to pressure her into hosting me. If only my cell phone had a voice activated option to help me find some answers. That wouldn't happen for another few years. What would I do in the meantime? I remembered seeing an old hotel near the Oyster House. I could camp out there for a few days until I figured out what to do next.

An hour later, I parked in front of the Admiral Fell Inn, a historic hotel commemorating the Fell family who founded Fell's Point in 1730. On a cobbled street corner, seven buildings made up

His Second Chance

the inn. As a former boarding house for sailors, their ghosts apparently lingered around even years later.

I walked inside the four-story, red brick building and approached the dark cherry front desk in the lobby, dragging my suitcases behind me.

Behind the counter, a tall man wearing a dark suit acknowledged me. "How can I help you tonight?"

"I need a room for a few nights," I told him.

"A king-sized bed?" he questioned as he tapped a keyboard in front of him.

"Yeah, that would be great."

"That'll be $531," he stated. "How will you be paying for it?"

I reached into my wallet and handed him a credit card. Gulping in a nervous breath, I willed it to work as he inserted it into his card reader. It was hard to tell if my card would still process, a fallout from time traveling.

A moment later, the desk clerk handed me my card and a room key covered by a cardboard jacket. "Your room number is on the inside of this envelope. Have a great stay with us. Breakfast tomorrow is at 6:30 a.m."

"Thank you." I turned from him and headed toward the elevator.

* * * *

The next morning, I sent Maggie a Facebook message: I'm staying in Fells Point. I can't wait to see

His Second Chance

you. I gave her my cell number and waited for a call. Good thing I typed everything out. Internally, I fought so hard to remember what I talked about when I was with her. Being with her made me tongue tied. I always wanted to say something I knew I shouldn't and that got in the way of expressing normal things.

While I waited for Maggie to call, I inspected my phone. Good thing I kept the same number, otherwise I wasn't sure how the time continuum would work when I traveled in time. I still didn't understand how or why I jumped from different parts of my life, but I learned to accept that I was at the mercy of something unknown. Thankful I hadn't jumped in a few days, I loved spending extra time with Maggie.

I scrolled through my contacts and found Prashant. Dialing his number, I hoped the connection worked.

"Hey man," he said into the phone.

Whew. A sigh of relief escaped my lips.

"What're you doing?" I asked.

"Manju and I are taking the baby to a holiday festival," he replied.

Another sigh of relief. They were still together. And their family was getting back to normal with little Taj. Everything would be perfect once Gia was born.

Prashant spoke again, "We're heading out right now. Can I call you back tomorrow?"

"Yeah, of course," I answered. "Call me when you're free."

"Will do, Ryan," Prashant said. "Later." He hung up the phone.

His Second Chance

I couldn't ask for a better friend. In undergrad, Prashant and I spent many weeknights over pizza discussing Stephen Hawking's black hole theories and weekends competing at his fraternity house trying to pick up the few cute girls on campus. I hated to admit that I usually won the battles. But Prashant won the war when he married Manju. They had so much in common that it made me gag. Admittedly, I was jealous, because I wanted the same thing. With Maggie.

My phone buzzed, jerking me from my thoughts. Maggie was calling.

As a huge grin emerged on my face, I answered the phone.

"Hi Ryan," Maggie cooed. "I'm so glad you gave me your number. I was about to give you mine because sending Facebook messages back and forth is brutal."

"Yeah it is," I agreed. "Listen, are you free this week? I want to see you."

"I can't tonight," Maggie sighed. "I have my kids. Actually, I have them all week."

"Is there any way you could get a sitter for an evening?" I suggested. "If money is an issue, I can help you pay for it."

"Yeah, let me check," she replied. "What did you have in mind?"

"The usual," I chuckled. "Dinner. Drinks. Horse and carriage ride under a heavy blanket so we can snuggle."

Maggie giggled. "Sounds like a great idea. I'll find a sitter."

I couldn't wait to spend time with her. I imagined that those wavy lines, like in the desert, followed her around. Like a mirage.

His Second Chance

Other men didn't think she was real if they passed her on the sidewalk.

"Where are you staying in Fells Point, anyway?" she asked.

"At the Admiral Fell Inn," I told her.

"That's a few blocks away from me. What kind of room do you have?" she purred.

"A king-sized bed," I half-whispered.

"We could make good use of it one night this week," Maggie bantered.

Instantly, my cock swelled. "I have plans for every corner."

"I can't wait," Maggie giggled again.

"Me either," I said. "Let me know when you're free."

Chapter 27

A few days later, I walked to Maggie's house to pick her up for dinner. She had arranged to have her kids stay overnight with a family friend. When she opened the front door, I gasped.

"What?" She patted her face a few times. "Do I have something on my cheek?"

"No ... No ... " I sputtered, still trying to form my words without stuttering like a fool. "You look ... amazing."

She wore a white V-neck cashmere sweater, a black suede skirt that came a couple inches above her bare knees, and spiked, tall, black boots. My mind wandered to those boots scraping against my bare back, leaving deep scratches, as Maggie wrapped her legs around me while I pushed my hard cock into her. Those boots alone were enough to fuel a week of wet dreams.

"Thank you." She blushed. "Let me get my jacket. Please come in."

His Second Chance

I followed Maggie into her living room, toward a coat closet. She pulled a long, leather jacket off the rack. Before she had a chance to put it on, I grasped it out of her hands and opened it up for her.

"Thank you again," she said, as she buttoned the coat. Her blonde hair tumbled into soft waves over the collar. "It's nice that someone has good manners."

"I will do whatever it takes to make you happy," I told her. "I promise."

"I believe you," she replied. I hoped it gave her tremendous confidence in life to realize she could have such an effect on someone.

When Maggie turned to face me, I cupped her chin in my hands, leaned into her, and kissed her beautiful mouth. That ravishing mouth. I was pretty much a puppet on her string. Sometimes she didn't even comprehend it.

"You are beautiful," I uttered. "So beautiful."

Maggie blushed and sheepishly turned away. "Thank you."

"I love that all of the other guys in the room stare at you when we go places," I stated. "It makes me feel ten feet tall."

"Where are we headed?" she asked me.

"Are you up for a walk to Little Italy?"

Maggie grimaced. "Not in these boots. That's a good mile away."

I chuckled at her self-deprecation. Sometimes she was a tough read. I remembered a time where we were on a date in undergrad and she told me after the fact that she wanted me to think about doing naughty things to her but didn't let on at all while we were out. She puzzled me.

"Then we'll get a cab," I said. "No worries." I shepherded Maggie out of the house and we walked past her neighbors' houses toward Fleet Street. Cars and vans whirred along the busy road. I walked on the outside of the sidewalk, holding Maggie's hand in mine.

As we approached the congested intersection, Maggie lifted a hand to her mouth and pinched two fingers between her lips. She blew out a high-pitched whistle toward an approaching taxi. I stared at her, my mouth agape. The cab screeched to a halt a dozen yards ahead of us.

"How did I not know you could do that?" I gawked at her, amazed at her skills.

"I have a lot of hidden talents." She winked at me and dropped me where I stood.

My insides groaned, fantasizing of what she might do to me later in my hotel room.

We strode toward the waiting cab and I opened the back door for her. She scooted in before me and I grabbed the door closed behind me as I settled next to her.

"Where to?" the cabbie asked us, while gawking at Maggie in his rearview mirror. I slid closer to her, giving the scruffy-haired man a silent claim on my prize.

"Sabatino's in Little Italy," I told him.

The cab advanced in and out of traffic along Fleet Street, passing a bakery, a handful of restaurants, and a bank. A few of the

HIS SECOND CHANCE

establishments twinkled with strings of holiday lights. Then the taxi made a right onto Caroline Street, and the next left onto Eastern Avenue. Two blocks later, a large, lit-up metal script sign saying "Little Italy" strung across the avenue.

As we entered the old, quaint Italian neighborhood, more colorful metal lanterns stretched from one side of the narrow road to the other, illuminating small cafes and decades-old family-run restaurants. Where the neighboring *medigans* lacked in holiday decorations, the Italians went over the top. Multi-colored Christmas trees flanked every door. Windows burst with string lights casting silhouettes. A white strand above us fizzled out and went black.

Red, white, and green banners gave shelter to large nativity scenes. With all of the exorbitant lighting, the neighborhood could be seen from a satellite. We made a right onto High Street.

We passed more row homes and closed-up bocce courts along High Street. The tall steeple of St. Leo's church beckoned us from a block away.

Two streets later, the taxi screeched to a halt at the corner of High and Fawn Streets. A large twinkling star stretched across the road above us, anchoring at a two-story green and white sign that read "Sabatino's" in vertical, block, red letters.

As Maggie and I exited the cab, a light snow fell. A few flakes stuck in her hair, giving her an angelic air. Her cheeks and nose were already red from being out in the cold. The sight of her took my breath away.

I shuttled Maggie into the small alcove of the main entrance of the restaurant. We approached the host stand and a stout, dark-haired woman guarded the dining room like it was the entrance to the Vatican.

"Good evening," she stoically greeted us. "Do you have a reservation?" The woman's mouth remained steady in a flat line.

"Yes," I answered. "Under Ryan, for two."

The woman grabbed a couple of black leather menus and said, "Follow me."

Inside the former row house, families and couples filled Sabatino's dining room at white-linened tables. Massive, vintage, black and white photographs of people adorned the walls. I assumed the folks in the pictures were former residents of the cultural neighborhood, possibly the Sabatino family. At the far end of the room, floor-to-ceiling windows cast an interior glow from outside street lamps. An aroma of garlic and onions filled the air. A billowy tune by Al Martino provided background music.

The curt hostess led Maggie and me to a two-person table along the wall and laid the menus down. While I grabbed Maggie's coat and placed it on a hook behind her, she took a seat. Then I settled into the chair across from her. We silently watched as the hostess filled our water glasses with a carafe that had already been sweating on the table.

"Enjoy your meal," the woman said and scurried off.

"She seems like she's having a rough night," Maggie joked with a smile.

"Maybe someone stole all of the butter for the bread baskets," I offered. "That could be chaos in a place like this. Someone might need to call the mafia."

Maggie giggled and leaned across the table, sealing our private joke.

Blood flowed throughout my body, happy that I could make Maggie laugh. I grasped her hand in mine.

"I've missed you so much," I told her.

"You saw me the other day," she replied. She opened her menu and I followed suit.

"Yeah, but before that," I stated. "I don't ever want to be without you again."

"Me neither," Maggie added. "I never realized how much I wanted to be with you until these past few days. I'd be at home doing everyday things and you'd pop into my head and I'd wonder what you're doing." She smiled at me. "I'd want to stop what I was doing and be with you."

"You are so great," I said. "I can't imagine my life without you in it. You make me so happy."

A smiling woman dressed in similar attire as the hostess approached our table. "Hi, my name is Nicole and I'll be your server tonight. Can I start you off with some wine?" She laid a basket full of warm bread in front of us.

"Yes!" Maggie answered for us. Then she acknowledged me. "Is white okay with you? Chardonnay?"

"Yes, whatever you want," I said.

Nicole spoke, "Perfect. I'll get that for you right away. Would you like an appetizer to start off?"

"Do you want to share prosciutto and melon?" I asked Maggie, while perusing my menu.

His Second Chance

"That sounds great," she replied.

Nicole spoke again, "I'll put that order in for you and then I'll come back and take your entree order." She turned and left Maggie and me alone.

As we talked across the table, I focused on Maggie's beautiful face. Occasionally, her leg grazed against mine in a way that could be written off as accidental, but I remained hopeful that it wasn't. My blood flowed into my crotch every time we made contact.

"Do I have something on my face?" Maggie softly poked her cheek with a finger.

"No. Why?"

"Because that guy two tables over to your left keeps staring at me," she confessed. "Like I'm a freak or something."

I casually peered to my left seeking out the voyeur and chuckled.

"He doesn't think you're a freak," I stated. "He's staring at you because he thinks you're hot." I smiled in pride that I was the envy of the man.

"Oh, come on," Maggie protested.

"It's true," I expressed. "You're the hottest woman in the room and he's checking you out. I would be too."

Maggie blushed and pulled at my heartstrings at the same time. She had no idea how gorgeous she was.

For the next hour, Maggie and I dined on penne with vodka sauce and shrimp parmigiana. We chatted nonstop about her kids, my family, and our mutual friends. She was a special woman and everyone who knew her was better for it.

His Second Chance

I avoided talking details about an occupation since I didn't want to tell her that I had no idea how long I would be in 2009. I stayed in this time period for almost a week and didn't grasp why I *wasn't* jumping. Was I permanently stuck in Baltimore now? What was the difference? Was it because nothing had exploded around me recently?

When would I travel through time again? If ever?

HIS SECOND CHANCE

Chapter 28

After dinner, Maggie and I left Sabatino's and sauntered across the street to Chiapparelli's to get some late-night drinks. The eatery was one of Little Italy's best-known and most-loved restaurants in Baltimore.

Inside, we settled in leather chairs at the far end of the green, marble-topped bar. Next to us, two sets of French doors separated the dining room from the bar. A few patrons nursed their beers at the tables behind us. Maggie sat so close to me that her boots grazed my legs. Oh, those seductive boots. I couldn't wait to do naughty things to her later that night.

With a couple of tumblers of Maker's Mark in front of us a few minutes later, I leaned into Maggie, closing the already-small space between us.

"You smell so good," I whispered.

"I sprayed my perfume ... right here." Maggie slowly ran a finger along her delicate neck.

His Second Chance

She owned me with that statement. Like no one had ever owned me before. I blew out a suggestive sigh.

"It's a pity I have to share you with the public," I spoke softly, inches from her ear.

With the back of the chair as a blocker, Maggie discreetly skimmed her fingers along my thigh, so that no one else in the bar could see what she did.

My cock hardened instantly.

"You're killin' me," I bantered.

"I know," Maggie replied, taking a sip of her whiskey.

"I want to fuck you tonight," I talked low and matter-of-factly.

"Is that so?" Maggie winked at me and flashed a wanton smile. She swallowed a mouthful of her whiskey while maintaining eye contact with me above the rim of her glass.

She knew exactly what she did to me and she teased me until I was at the brink of grabbing her by the hand and pulling her into the restroom for a quickie.

"Oh yes," I replied, imbibing my bourbon. "All night. I hope you're up for it."

"I wouldn't miss it," Maggie purred.

A wavy lock of her blonde hair fell into her cheek and I brushed it back.

"Thank you," she said.

"I did that so that I could touch your beautiful face," I replied. "You are the most stunning woman I have ever met."

Maggie blushed with an innocent smile and faced away from me.

His Second Chance

"I bet you say that to all the pretty girls," she spoke.

"Only one," I said, nodding to her. "No one else ever deserved it."

Maggie pulled another strand of flaxen hair away from her head and curled it around her finger. "So, I'm The One?"

"The One--and only," I confirmed. "You make me love like I've never loved before. And you have this way of making me speak right from the heart. I've never been comfortable doing that with anyone before, or after, you."

"I feel the same way," she said. "Everything is so easy with you. So effortless. We get along so well. You're my best friend. I can tell you anything."

"There's no one I would rather be with," I said as I finished my drink. "I have everything I want and need." Internally, I prayed that I wouldn't jump again any time soon. I willed the time-travel gods to keep me grounded. I would offer up a small sacrifice if I could stay with Maggie forever.

Maggie swallowed the rest of her liquor. "What do you say we get outta here?"

I motioned toward the bartender who had been hovering at the far end of the bar washing glasses. "Check please!"

After paying the bill, I followed Maggie out of the restaurant with my hand at the small of her back. My heart thumped like a woodpecker inside my chest. I couldn't wait to touch the rest of her body beneath me.

Outside, we hailed another taxi and made a beeline for my hotel.

His Second Chance

The entire cab trip had me thinking about doing naughty things with her sitting over there in the passenger seat. I continuously fought to lower my expectations about her intentions. Nervous that she might not be thinking the same thing I was, I continued talking with her and making her laugh as we rode. I loved her laugh. It boosted my ego. Nothing sexier than a hot woman who laughed at my jokes.

At the hotel, I pulled Maggie into the elevator, then up against me, and kissed her mouth, her cheeks, and her face. My hands wandered all over her body and I held her close to me. I missed kissing her so much. Her lips were warm and soft like nothing I had ever experienced before. I could kiss her for days, but my body told my mind to keep moving.

When the doors opened, we rushed to my room, hand in hand. With Maggie against me, I fumbled with the key fob at the door and finally pushed it open.

In the foyer of the room, I yanked Maggie's long jacket off and tossed it on the floor. With her jacket out of the way, I thrust her against the wall, facing me. I steadied her hips with both of my hands and knelt in front of her. As if I examined a rare piece of fine art, I meticulously lifted Maggie's skirt, exposing her bare thighs. The sudden change in speed elicited a giggle out of Maggie's mouth. She stayed still while I traced a finger along the inside of her leg, heading toward the top.

I stared up at Maggie, sending her an unspoken signal that I would give her intense sensual gratification. She beamed back at me.

His Second Chance

I raised Maggie's skirt to her waist, exposing a pair of white lace panties. With a hook of my finger, I pulled the panties to the side to reveal her pink pussy. I leaned into Maggie, sucking her luscious lips with mine. Her body would be mine and I could take my sweet time with it.

"Oh my god," Maggie whispered.

With one hand on her ass and the other keeping her panties at bay, I plunged my tongue deep inside Maggie, lapping every sweet juice.

Frustrated that my path wasn't clear, I grasped the sides of her panties and pushed them to the floor. Maggie's bare pussy was the most dazzling thing I ever witnessed. I lapped her again, my hands on her ass pushing her toward me.

The moans escaping her mouth confirmed to me that Maggie enjoyed what I gave her. She laid a boot-covered leg over my shoulder, her hint of what she wanted next.

With my arms behind her, I unzipped her skirt from the back, shifted her leg from my shoulder, and pushed Maggie's skirt to the floor. I slid the front of my body up along hers, stopping at her neck. As I kissed her silken skin, I grabbed her hips and pulled her up into me, lifting her off the floor. Instinctively, Maggie wrapped her boots around my waist and I carried her to my bed.

Sitting upright on the bed, Maggie pawed at my clothes, yanking off my button-down shirt and threw it on the floor. She quickly unbuckled my belt and unzipped my jeans, allowing more space for my hardening cock.

"I need you so bad," she whispered in a deep, sultry voice.

His Second Chance

Maggie slipped her hand into my waistband, and my cock stretched towards her. It had a mind of its own, wanting to be in her sexy grasp. My stomach sucked in without me even thinking, to provide her better access.

"You are so hard for me," she said.

"You have no idea," I told her.

As she let go of me, I grasped the lower edge of her sweater in my hands and lifted it over her head. I reached behind her and unhooked her bra. She sat naked in front of me, except for her boots.

"Keep your boots on," I instructed her.

Maggie pushed my jeans and boxers to the floor as I kicked off my shoes. I leaned into her on the bed, pushing her upward toward the center. She bent her knees, pulling her legs upward and then over my shoulders. The spike heels of her boots lightly scratched my back, giving me carnal pleasure.

Hovering over her, I steadied my thick cock above her pussy, the tip grazing her for a moment.

"Please don't tease me," she spoke low. "I want you inside me."

"Your wish is my command," I said. "Give me one second."

After I grabbed a condom and deftly put it on, I pushed my hard cock inside easily inside her and thrust into her. Maggie was dripping wet, the inside of her thighs glistened. A grunt left my lips. She felt amazing around me; her muscles constricting my shaft.

"Oh my god," she whispered. "I can feel every inch of you."

"You do this to me," I told her.

His Second Chance

I plunged into Maggie again and again, thrusting up and down, as her boots scraped my back. The conflicting combination of pain and pleasure sent me into an erotic spiral. Kissing her mouth and silken neck, I pumped into her. Maggie's arms were all over me, grasping anything she could hold onto.

I knew I couldn't last much longer so I slid out of her, despite her protests and efforts to lock me against her with her legs. Lying next to her, I struggled to regain my breath. Before I could, however, she rolled over onto me, facing away from me. Her soft, wet pussy slid along my hard cock as she pushed herself against me. The heels of her boots dug gently and sexily into my ribs as she reached for my yearning cock and slid it inside of her.

Nothing could stop me from feeling so good. Maggie moaned as she rode me slow and hard. I decided that if she would make me explode so soon, two could play that game. My strong hands slid from her calves to her thighs and over her sexy backside as I grabbed her hips and pulled myself up into her hard. And deep.

"Oh my god, baby," she cried out. "Please don't stop. I'm so close."

No chance of that. My back arched and my hips bucked hard up into her hot, wet pussy as we thrusted against each other.

"God, baby, I'm right. There. Oh. God. Ohhhhh," she cried as my balls tightened. "I want to feel your cock pulse inside of me as you cum." That's all I could handle. My cock went into overdrive and my hips pushed so hard up against her as I exploded so hard that I ached.

His Second Chance

"Mmmmm," was her sultry response to my orgasm, and it somehow made me keep pulsing inside of her. Maggie fell back onto me and I wrapped my arms tightly around her as I buried my kisses in the nape of her neck. I was so intoxicated by her.

We kissed and held each other for what seemed like forever until our bodies succumbed to exhausted sleep.

His Second Chance

Chapter 29

For the next three weeks, Maggie and I spent almost every day together. She wasn't ready to introduce me to Madelyn and Thomas yet, so we'd meet for lunch, have mini dates at the grocery store when she needed a jug of milk, or enjoy a quick walk through Inner Harbor absorbing the holiday decorations. We took every opportunity to stand close to each other on crowded sidewalks, with my arm around her shoulders, as snow fell onto her eyelashes.

One night, when Maggie secured a babysitter, we took a sunset cruise, even though the outside temperature was in the low 40s. She and I snuggled under a blanket and held hands. We made out while the sun splattered the sky in beautiful pink, orange, and yellow hues.

Another night, I secretly met Maggie at the library while her kids needed to do some research for their book reports. A few other patrons filled the main floor pulling books out of tall shelves. A low murmur of voices filled the open area. Librarians stood at large desks helping bibliophiles search for their next favorite novel.

His Second Chance

From a table at the far end of the room pretending to read a magazine, I watched quietly as Maggie helped her kids find books and resources for their projects. She huddled over them and guided them along. I always knew she would be a great mom. And I was right.

`Meet me near the restrooms on the 3rd floor,` I texted her.

When her phone pinged, she reached for it in her pocket. Without glancing in my direction, she smiled broadly, realizing what I wanted.

She told her kids, "I'll be back in a few minutes. Heading to the ladies' room."

"Okay, Mom," Madelyn and Thomas echoed. Madelyn was the spitting image of her mom with blonde curly hair and jade eyes. In a few years, she'll be fighting the boys off. Thomas lacked a few teeth in his mouth but it didn't stop him from smiling wide.

Two minutes later, Maggie found me outside the ladies' room on the third floor. I stared at her with the eyes of a wolf.

"Nobody's in there." I nodded to the door. "I already checked."

"What did you have in mind?" she begged the question.

Without a word, I grabbed Maggie's hand and snatched her inside. She giggled in response. Once we stepped in the restroom, I locked the door from the inside. I pushed Maggie against the nearest wall, her back to me. I enclosed her tiny body, touching every inch of her with my warmth. Inching my mouth near Maggie's ear, I whispered, "I want you so bad."

We stood like that for a moment, absorbing the sensual heat.

His Second Chance

Then I broke the hold and turned Maggie toward me.

In two steps, Maggie rested against the wide sink counter, her eyes bore into mine. She wore a long sweater and a black leggings that hugged her beautiful curves. Lucky me.

I sidled up in front of Maggie and twisted her body around so that she faced the mirror. She planted her hands on the edge of the counter as I stood behind her and yanked her leggings and panties down. With my mouth kissing every inch of her warm neck, I handed her a condom packet out of my pocket. As she fumbled getting it out of the wrapper, I unbuckled my belt and jeans. She handed me the unwrapped condom and I slid it on my hard and ready cock.

In the mirror, she locked eyes with me and bent forward, letting the tip of my cock part her hot wet lips. Groaning and swelling, I think my eyes closed themselves to try to lessen the pleasure of the moment.

With one hand around her torso and the other on the counter to steady us, I bucked into Maggie from behind. Harder. Deeper. Faster. Maggie's quick, shallow breaths indicated that she savored every push. Watching her blissful face in the mirror nearly made me pass out.

"This is so hot," she moaned.

"I couldn't keep my eyes off you downstairs," I puffed out. "I had to have you."

With one last, robust thrust, I exploded while inside her. I collapsed against Maggie, holding her in my arms. Every ounce of my energy left me. I held her for a minute more, then we hastily

His Second Chance

adjusted our clothing as if nothing happened and scurried out of the restroom.

* * * *

A few days before Christmas, Maggie and I feasted on crabs at Captain James Seafood Palace in Canton, two blocks east of Fells Point. Inside the merchant-vessel-shaped restaurant, we sat across from each other at a brown paper covered table. The aroma of sea water and the secret ingredients in Old Bay filled the air. Wooden mallets lay in front of us. We shared a dozen large crabs, smothered in J.O. Spice, with a side of coleslaw.

"I can't believe I wore white," Maggie lamented, her hands covered in sauce and melted butter. She carefully held her arms in front of her white sweatshirt, like how surgeons don't want to touch anything after scouring their hands for surgery. "What was I thinking?"

"You're fine." I smiled at her. Even with a pile of discarded crustacean shells in front of her, Maggie looked adorable. I loved staring at her, with the bonus that she was stunning. "If you get any on your clothes, I'll help you undress."

"Although the offer is tempting, we don't have time for that," she sighed. "I only have the sitter for two hours."

"You'd be amazed what I can do under pressure." I winked at her.

Maggie giggled while taking a bite of crab in her sticky fingers.

His Second Chance

"I know you told me before that you want to spend Christmas with your kids and I'm fine with that," I began, "but what about New Year's? Do you think you can get a sitter for then? Even overnight? I'd love to spend it with you."

Not spending Christmas with Maggie killed me, but I respected her wishes. I had no idea what it was like to be a single parent, but I didn't envy her situation of doing the right thing for her kids and sacrificing her love life. Madelyn was eleven now and Thomas was nine. Even though I saw them at the library, I wanted to meet them but couldn't risk interrupting their lives while wondering if and when I would travel in time again. That wasn't fair to them.

"Already taken care of. My kids are spending the night at their friends'." Maggie whacked a crab with her mallet. "What did you have in mind?"

"Great! We can get a nice dinner, then Inner Harbor has ice skating if you want to do that," I offered. By pulling money out of my 401k, I was able to stay longer at the hotel. The penalty was worth it. I still had no idea when I would jump again, so I needed to savor every moment with Maggie and not worry about finances.

"Yes, I'd love it," Maggie said.

"We've already had Italian and now we're having crabs," I stated. "Do you want to do something different? You know this city better than I do. You tell me."

"How about Tio Pepe? It's a great old Spanish place on East Franklin. They have *fantastic* sangria and a pine nut cake that's to die for," Maggie gushed. I swear her mouth salivated at the notion. "You have to try it."

His Second Chance

"Whatever you want, babe," I stated with a toothy grin. Making Maggie happy was at the top of my priorities. If she wanted to spend New Years in a hole-in-the-wall pizza shop drinking beers or going to the ballet, I was all for it. As long as I was with her. "I'll make reservations."

HIS SECOND CHANCE

Chapter 30

At 7:00 on New Year's Eve, Maggie and I hustled out of the almost-full parking garage across the street from Tio Pepe rushing to get to our dinner reservation. With her hand in mine, we dodged oncoming holiday traffic along East Franklin Street. Snow started to fall, creating a perfect holiday night.

Before we stepped inside the red awning of the restaurant's entrance, I pulled Maggie close to me and stole a sweet kiss. Under her long leather jacket, she wore a black wrap dress that dipped into a low V on her chest. I couldn't wait to discover what was underneath it.

I grabbed the door of the restaurant and held it open as Maggie stepped inside. The landmark eatery had been serving Spanish Continental fare since 1968. We descended four steps from the street into a time capsule of a restaurant. The decor hadn't changed in decades. At the front edge of the white brick dining room, a stout man in a black suit greeted us at the host station.

His Second Chance

"Good evening," he said to us. "Happy New Year. Do you have a reservation?"

"Yes," I replied. "It's under Ryan. I'm so sorry we're a few minutes late."

"It's no problem." The maître d' scanned his list of holiday diners and found our reservation. "Please follow me."

We trailed the host through a small room filled with round and square tables covered in white linen, each surrounded by brown rattan chairs. Other clientele dined on gazpacho, paella, and Tio Pepe's famous suckling pig. Pitchers of red and white sangria complemented each meal. Twinkling white string lights wrapped around green leaf boughs hung from the archways. A dozen poinsettias scattered around the room. A tall Christmas tree decorated in silver ornaments and a luminous star glistened in the corner.

As Maggie and I sat down and placed our orders, I ogled Maggie a little longer than usual. "You look beautiful tonight." She could launch a thousand ships. My most anticipated moment was literally at hand as I leaned across the table and kissed her soft and warm mouth. Those lips. They blanked my mind every time I touched them with mine.

"Thank you." Maggie blushed. God, she was so cute when she did that. My eyes wandered to her bare neck and the lovely dress a few inches below it. Then the thought hit me.

"Did you still want to go ice skating tonight?" I inquired. "I mean, will you be able to in that dress?"

His Second Chance

Maggie slapped a hand to her forehead. "I completely forgot we planned to do that when I got dressed earlier."

"It's okay," I reassured her. "We can do something else. Are you still up for Inner Harbor?"

"Yes," she answered. "That would be fun!"

While Maggie dined on Spanish prawns in curry sauce, I ate chicken sautéed in olive oil with peppers and tomatoes. A carafe of white sangria nestled on the table between us.

As I forked up some tomatoes, a few fell rogue and landed on my lap.

"Ugh, I'm such a slob," I lamented, trying to make light of my lackluster dining skills.

"That's okay," Maggie replied. "I still love you anyway." She casually took a sip of her fruit-infused wine.

Wait. What did she just say? Did she say she loved me? Maggie's response and attitude were so flippant, as if she said it a thousand times. But she never did. I would have remembered it. I know I would have. But I didn't want to make a big deal of it now in case I misheard her. But what if she meant every word? She and I were perfect together. Maggie and I fit; I couldn't explain it. She had personality, compassion, and kindness. She was smart, funny, and driven. She and I could talk about anything. Maggie was everything I never expected to find in a woman. I couldn't be without her again. Maggie gave me life. She made me full. I was a better man for having found that love. She made me feel good enough. Plus, she was hot. So hot.

His Second Chance

All that made me think. Had I never told Maggie I loved her? I was pretty sure I did, because I did indeed love her. What a chump I was if I never told her. I needed to remedy that before I traveled in time again. Whenever that was.

After eating pine nut cake and drinking another carafe of sangria, I paid the bill and we headed out. As Maggie and I stepped onto the sidewalk, more snow began to fall. A perfect complement to the night.

"Are you okay to walk a little bit to get to Inner Harbor?" I asked Maggie, eyeing up her black heels. "We'll never get a cab. Not tonight."

"Yes, I'll be fine," she said. "Maybe we can stop at a pub along the way and take a break."

"I was thinking the same thing." I beamed at her and slid an arm around her shoulders. "Let's go."

Arm in arm, we sauntered down South Charles Street taking in the crowd of people with the same idea. We passed boutique shops and breakfast cafes closed up for the night. Modern skyscrapers mixed in amongst three-story buildings. Old St. Paul's Church offered sanctuary from the snow in its red brick archways. Internal lights illuminated the second-story stained glass window, sending a kaleidoscope of colors into the night sky.

Two blocks later, we stopped in front of the Lord Baltimore Hotel, its omnipotence poised next to us. Built in 1928, the elegant hotel had the honor of being the tallest building in the state of Maryland back then.

"Let's go in there and get a drink," Maggie suggested.

His Second Chance

I followed her through the revolving door and we found our way to the dark lounge. Almost every man in the room snuck a peek at Maggie, much to the chagrin of their dates. I beamed with pride that I was the arm candy of the hottest woman in the building.

We settled at the bar and caught the attention of the mixologist. He handed us a list of holiday specials.

"What do you want tonight?" Maggie cooed as we glanced over the drink menu.

"What I want isn't something I can have right now," I talked low enough only for her to hear.

"Later. I promise," she whispered.

My insides burned with desire. If I planned on staying up all night with her, I needed some caffeine.

"I'm still deciding, so you go first," Maggie stated while perusing the drink list.

I spoke loud enough for the bartender to take notice of me, "I'll have a Maker's Mark mixed with Red Bull on the rocks."

"Sure thing," the barkeep replied then turned his attention to Maggie. "And you, miss?"

"I'll have a candy cane martini," Maggie answered and handed him back the drink menu. He turned from us and amalgamated our refreshments.

"Have I told you tonight how gorgeous you are?" I leaned into Maggie and whispered in her ear.

"Yes, but you can tell me as often as you want." She placed her hand on my thigh and the skin underneath my pants burned to her touch.

His Second Chance

Sitting next to her intoxicated me. With alcohol, I found license to put my hand on her thigh while we talked closely. I could feel it burning through her pants and she leaned to talk close to my ear so we could hear each other above the rising din from the other patrons at the bar.

"I can't wait to get you out of those clothes," I whispered.

"It'll be a Happy New Year for both of us." Maggie winked at me.

A moment later, the bartender interrupted us and presented our drinks. We shifted our bodies so that we didn't give him the impression that we would get naked in front of him—even though the lustful idea was on my mind.

After our second drink, Maggie put her hand on top of my hand which lay on her leg and pressed it down lightly, moving it an inch higher on her thigh. I could swear I touched some kind of extra texture where my hand now rested. Again, blood left my brain and headed south, making it uncomfortable to move.

For the next half hour, Maggie and I talked and laughed over drinks, both of us getting a refill. Spending time with her met all of my needs and wants. She asked the right questions, kept me on my toes with her wicked humor, and asked me about myself. Even though she knew almost everything about me, I still couldn't tell her how I traveled in time. I had no idea how to. Hell, Prashant barely believed me and he was a scientist. In the meantime, I wanted to savor every moment with Maggie because I didn't know when it would be my last.

His Second Chance

At 10:00, Maggie snatched the bill from the bartender before I had a chance to pay it. "My treat."

"Thank you." I blushed. She never ceased to amaze me.

"Maybe it's time for us to go," she said softly into my ear. I was a goner. Thank god she stood up and went to the restroom after that. The uncomfortable bulge in my pants forced me to physically reach into my pocket and shift it into a more agreeable position within my boxer briefs.

Moments later, Maggie and I headed out the door and into the New Year's Eve crowd who carried horns, wore shiny hats, and blared noisemakers heading to parties at different venues around Baltimore. Large colorful banners hung from the outside of buildings proclaiming, "Happy New Year 2010!"

His Second Chance

Chapter 31

Hand in hand, Maggie and I maneuvered our way through the mass of holiday revelers along East Pratt Street toward Inner Harbor. Laughing people jostled us, but we didn't mind. The street was blocked off to vehicle traffic as hordes of partiers swarmed the avenue, scoping out local pubs and restaurants for small concerts and balloon drops. Boats decorated in lights and decorations filled the glistening inlet.

At 11:45, the stationary crowd of people in the harbor's red brick plaza prevented us from getting closer to the water. Even though Maggie wasn't dressed for it, we stopped at the temporary seasonal wall of the Inner Harbor Ice Rink and observed other skaters bundled up in puffer jackets, scarves, and hats.

"We can come back another day," I told her.

"I'd love that," Maggie gushed.

I took her hand in mine and leaned closer to her. "I've had such an awesome night with you. Not only tonight, but ever since I came to Baltimore."

"Me too," she spoke low. Her beautiful green eyes sparkled in the night. "I've never been happier. I love spending time with you. You make me believe that I can do anything."

"You *can* do anything. You're amazing. I have everything I want and need with you." I held Maggie close to me and kissed her soft lips. Those wonderful lips. She broke our hold.

"Why did it take so long for us to get together?" she asked the lingering question.

"I don't know," I told her. "But I never want to be without you again."

"Me either," she said.

I pulled Maggie close to me again and positioned my mouth next to her ear. "I love you." A crowd of thousands around us wasn't the most private place to tell her, but I couldn't wait another moment.

Maggie gasped and jerked her head back. "What did you say? Did you say what I think you just said?" Her wide eyes bore into mine and her mouth dropped into an O.

"Yes," I reaffirmed her. "I love you."

"I ... I ... I'm sorry I sound stunned. ... It's just ... it's just ... you never said that to me before," she squealed in delight.

"Seriously?" I questioned. "I never told you that? I thought maybe I did and I forgot."

"Not once," she replied. "A girl remembers the first time a guy tells her he loves her. Over the years, you've told me I'm adorable and that you like me and that I am sexy when I'm passionate, but you've never told me you *loved* me."

His Second Chance

"Let me fix that right now." I took Maggie's rosy cheeks in my hands, inches from my face. "I love you with all my heart and soul. I never want to be with anyone but you. You make me so happy. I can't explain it. You make me feel whole, like I've never felt before. You are the love of my life and I will never let you get away from me again."

Maggie took the breath out of my lungs without even trying. With my job as a consultant, I told people all the time that they were in control of their own feelings, but Maggie was an exception to that rule for me. She made me experience so many things with only a simple phrase.

"You make me feel like a better version of me," I explained. "You make me feel desirable and good about myself. You remember things about my life and you take an interest in them. I have never had that with anyone else before you or since."

Under my palms, Maggie's face formed a wide grin. "I love you, too. I can tell you anything and you won't judge me. I love your lust for life. That you can take a mundane thing like going to a deli and making it fun. That you make everyone you encounter feel better about themselves. I love that you want to spend your time with me. You take me for who I am, with my flaws and all. I've been in love with you since the day I met you. But I always found it difficult to tell you because I never knew how you felt."

"You are perfect for me," I practically sang.

As I gazed into Maggie's mesmerizing, jade eyes, the crowd around us hummed louder getting ready for the stroke of midnight into the new year.

His Second Chance

On the other side of the harbor, a three-story screen which was attached to the exterior of the aquarium displayed a giant countdown. One minute to go.

I squeezed Maggie in my arms and held her tightly against me. Along with the rest of the crowd, we watched the numbers tick down. Thirty seconds to go.

The crowd around us buzzed louder, anticipating the celebration.

We all chanted: "Ten ... Nine ... Eight ... Seven ... Six ... Five ... Four ... Three ... Two ... One!"

A prismatic fireworks display shot up into the night sky, illuminating the entire harbor while the posse of merrymakers around us wished each other Happy New Year. I planted a kiss on Maggie's lips to celebrate. More pink, gold, and white pyrotechnic rockets flashed into the sky.

I gasped realizing what was happening. The last time something exploded over top of me, I traveled in time. I couldn't leave Maggie. Not tonight. Not ever. But fate was out of my hands. I squeezed her tighter than before and puffed out a nervous sigh.

"Oh, no."

"What's wrong?" Maggie uttered with a serious expression on her face. She must have picked up my change in demeanor and held my hand. "Are you okay?"

"I ... I ... I ..." Words escaped me as panic raced through my veins. What could I tell her? I still didn't know all the answers myself. "I'm okay," I finally managed to say. "Just promise me something."

HIS SECOND CHANCE

"Yes. Anything."

"Promise me you'll wait for me," I instructed.

"Ryan, what are you talking about?" Maggie dismissed me. "Wait for you for what?"

"I can't explain it. Someday I might be able to, but I can't right now," I disclosed. I squeezed Maggie again as I fought to keep a tear from escaping my eyes. I hated to leave her. Especially now. Especially tonight.

Maggie glared at me with unconvinced eyes. "You're being weird."

"Just promise, after tomorrow, you'll wait for me."

"Okay," she relented and then kissed me. "I promise you I'll wait."

HIS SECOND CHANCE

Chapter 32

The next morning, I stood in a familiar kitchen. Opposite me, a large print of the Hyderabad temples hung on the pristine white wall. Coffee brewed in a nearby pot. A few toys were scattered on the countertops.

Prashant's kitchen.

Voices from the hall caught my attention. Prashant and Manju's voices. A wave of relief swept over me that they were still together.

Before I could glance at my watch to determine the year, Manju walked into the kitchen, with Prashant a few steps behind her.

"Good morning, sleepyhead! We wondered when you were getting up," she called to me. Manju wore pink and yellow plaid pajama pants and a white Carnegie Mellon T-shirt. Her long dark hair was pulled loosely on top of her head.

"We've been up for two hours with the kids," Prashant added. His beard had been freshly trimmed and he wore baggy, black

His Second Chance

sweatpants and a matching T-shirt. "You missed Taj trying to bet his sister that he could shove a Lego up his nose."

"We had to separate them with the threat of force," Manju said.

"I tried to appeal to their sympathetic side by asking them why they would want to make me feel like I've failed as a parent," Prashant chuckled. "But that didn't work either." He glared at me over the top of his coffee cup. His brows bunched into a narrow V.

"What?" I whispered to Prashant as Manju crossed the kitchen to get another cup of coffee. We waited for her to exit the room.

"Don't fuck with me," he sneered. "You weren't here yesterday. Tell me what happened."

I chuckled. "It's complicated. I still can't figure it out myself.'

"I don't care if you're disproving Stephen Hawking's theories, I want to know." Prashant twirled the wedding ring around his finger and I sighed in relief that he was back together with Manju. "I'm your best friend. You tell me everything."

Manju wandered back in the kitchen and Prashant and I quickly hushed.

"What are you two boys conspiring?" She leered at us with suspicious eyes.

"How beautiful my wife is," Prashant sang.

"Good thing we met at Panther Hollow Inn that night," Manju replied, taking her husband's bait. "Otherwise, my mother might have tried to set me up on another blind date."

"What do you mean?" I asked. "When did she do that?"

"In 1998," Manju answered. "When I was at CMU getting my Masters."

His Second Chance

Prashant and I exchanged glances as Manju poured coffee into a mug for me.

She continued, "I was supposed to meet some guy that my mother arranged, I don't even remember his name, but I was late getting to the date and, by the time I arrived there 15 minutes late, he was gone."

"Why were you late?" I asked while reaching for cream and sugar on the table.

"I remember I had a 6:00 appointment with my professor, but some jerk jumped in front of me and made me late to the date. I didn't want to explain what happened to my mother and avoided talking to her for a couple of days."

"Who was your professor? Maybe I had him?" Prashant inquired.

"Randy Pausch," Manju replied. "I'm so glad I worked with him before he died. Great guy."

Oh my god. I was the reason why Prashant and Manju didn't meet that night. I was the one who jumped in front of her to see Dr. Pausch. That's why I saw her crying on the street corner then. She was upset that she let down her mother.

I was the jerk who squashed the butterfly.

* * * *

"Now that Manju is busy with the kids, you can tell me what happened." Prashant cornered me an hour later while Manju was out on a bike ride with Taj and Gia.

His Second Chance

"How long do you have?" I jested.

"Did you find Maggie or not?"

"Yes, in 2009," I answered. "But wait—what's today's date?"

"November 5, 2016," Prashant replied. "Do you want me to prove it?"

"Nah, I believe you," I stated with a flip of my hand. "In 2009, I dated this woman Rebecca. We lived together in D.C."

"Oh yeah, I remember her. Nice girl, but I never bought that you were head over heels for her."

I chuckled in agreement. "While I was there, I connected with Maggie on Facebook and found that she lived in Baltimore."

"Wow, what are the chances?" Prashant exclaimed. "Because wasn't she in Boston the last time?"

"Yes," I continued. "So, I drove to Baltimore and met Maggie for lunch and—" I still couldn't believe that that simple lunch spawned into something amazing with Maggie.

"And what?" Prashant held on to my every word.

"Long story short, I broke up with Rebecca and spent the next few weeks in Baltimore with Maggie. It was great. Best time of my life." My mind wandered to our fantastic time together. "I told her I loved her for the first time. Then on New Year's Eve, I lost her."

"What? What do you mean you *lost* her?"

"I mean I jumped again." I kneaded the scar on my right hand. "And I have no idea where she is now. I hope she's still in Baltimore but she could be anywhere."

"There's only one way to find out," Prashant answered.

We scurried into his office and flipped open his laptop. I logged into Facebook. To my good fortune, Maggie and I were still connected as Friends. Her "Current City" indicated Washington, D.C.

"I need to get to D.C. and find her!"

"Dude, you can't show up there unannounced," Prashant stopped me. "It's been what, seven years? You think it was yesterday, but *she* doesn't."

Shit. Prashant had a point. I hated when he was right.

Prashant continued, "You need a plan. Even if it's as simple as you say you're in town for work. Send her a message now and tell her you're in town."

"Good idea."

"I can take you to the train station and you can work out the details while you're on the road," Prashant offered.

"Thanks, man. I appreciate it."

I sent a message to Maggie: Hi! I'm sorry for the short notice, but I will be in D.C. tomorrow. Would you like to meet for dinner and drinks?

Within ten minutes, she replied: Yes. Where and when?

I wrote: How about Zaytinya at 7:00? It's right on the edge of Chinatown.

Maggie responded: I know where it is. Meet you there.

His Second Chance

Her terse response should have concerned me, but it didn't. I was just thrilled to see her again.

The next morning, I was on an Amtrak train headed to Washington, D.C.

Chapter 33

At 6:30, I hopped off the train and fought through the rush-hour crowd at Union Station. I found my way to the Red Line platform and boarded the Metro. The commuter train overflowed with nine-to-fivers from the Columbus Circle area. The seats were at capacity while many travelers steadied themselves in the aisle with overhead hand-grips. After a long day of traveling, I was tired, but excited to spend time with Maggie again.

Ten claustrophobic minutes later, I disembarked at the Gallery Place/Chinatown station and headed to Zaytinya. Strolling along G Street at dusk, the National Portrait Gallery and American Art Museum, with its tall roman columns, was on my left. A few people relaxed on its wide steps enjoying the late fall evening temperatures.

At the next intersection, the bright yellow, abstract Epoch Sculpture stood sentry-like in front of the Mediterranean restaurant. I pushed through the glass-windowed door and approached the host station.

His Second Chance

"Just one for dinner tonight?" the cute, dark-skinned hostess asked me from behind her podium.

"No," I answered. "I'm meeting someone. A woman."

"I seated a blonde woman a few minutes ago and she said she was expecting a man," the young woman stated. "Are you Ryan?"

"Yes, ma'am," I replied. My heart jumped that Maggie was a mere few feet away. I couldn't wait to see her.

"Come with me."

I followed the hostess through the labyrinth of brown tables and chairs and found Maggie seated at a white, high-backed booth. Instantly, my mouth formed in a huge smile as she caught my eye. Even seven years later, she was still so beautiful. Her blonde hair fell into waves on her shoulders. It was a few inches shorter, but complemented her. Maggie's green eyes sparkled above her glistening cheeks. I quickly glanced at her left hand resting on the table. No ring. I exhaled a sigh of relief that she didn't move on to someone else.

As I approached the booth, I leaned into Maggie and hugged her. She smelled so sweet, like fresh peaches on a hot July afternoon. "It's so good to see you." I released her and took a seat across from her.

"You too," she said. "How are you? What have you been up to?"

"I was with Prashant and his family recently," I answered, not touching the menu in front of me. I was too enamored with Maggie to decide what I wanted to eat. "They are in Pittsburgh and doing well. How about you?"

His Second Chance

"I'm good," she said. "Madelyn and Thomas are 18 and 16. Madelyn is a freshman at Georgetown so I visit her pretty often. And Thomas is a starting shortstop on his varsity baseball team."

"That's great!" That reminded me. "How did you come to be in D.C.? You were in Baltimore the last time I saw you."

Maggie grinned a cute smile. "A few years ago, I was offered an awesome job at the American Art Museum. I hated to move the kids again, but they were both on board."

"I walked by it getting here," I gushed. "No wonder you were familiar with this restaurant."

"This place has the best Mediterranean food in the area," Maggie replied as she flipped open her menu. I followed suit.

We ordered small plates of roasted eggplant, grape leaves, tahini, lamb, and chicken skewers with a complementary bottle of white wine. We split the entrees in half and shared everything, sometimes I grazed her hand with mine. Even though Maggie didn't object, she didn't go out of her way to touch mine.

I refilled Maggie's wine glass when I noticed it was near empty.

"That's okay," she said as she stopped me with a flat hand motion. "I don't need anymore."

"Why? Are you afraid you'll get drunk and jump me?" I jested.

Maggie scoffed. "No." She glanced away from me and then back again as if she was trying to figure out what to say. She pursed her lips and then finally spoke again, "Ryan, why are you here?"

"Because I wanted to see you," I responded.

"No, I mean why are you here *now*?" Maggie gazed away from me again. "You go MIA for seven years and now you act like we are dating again. Like nothing has changed." She faced me and narrowed her eyes. Her lips disappeared into a thin line, opposite of her usual cheerful face. I had never seen her so exasperated with me.

"Maggie ... I ... I ..." My words left me. What a shithead I was. Selfishly, I hadn't considered the fact that she might be mad at me for leaving her.

"You tell me on New Year's Eve how much you love me and then the next morning you're gone without even a note," she hissed. "What the hell ..."

"I asked you to wait for me," I proffered.

"How long did you expect me to wait?!" Maggie spat at me. "It's been seven years, Ryan. Seven years! I have a life. I have kids. I have a job. I stupidly believed that you'd get back in touch with me after a few weeks or even a month, but nothing. Then you show up after seven years and think we're good and can pick up where we left off. What the hell. Who does that?"

"Maggie, I can explain ..." I reached for her hand across the table but she quickly snatched it back. She had every right to be pissed at me. No wonder her message the day before was terse. If I didn't tell her the truth now, I would lose her for good. She might not believe me, but I had to try.

"Don't bother." Maggie shuffled her body in the booth as if to get up, but stuck to the leather seating.

"Maggie, please don't go." I reached for her across the table, stopping her. "Just give me ten minutes and I'll tell you the truth. If you still don't like what I say, then you have every right to leave me here and never speak to me again. Please. Just listen to me."

His Second Chance

Maggie puffed out a breath of confession. "Fine." She slowly settled back into the booth. "You have ten minutes."

As my heart hammered inside my chest, I inhaled deeply trying to quickly think of a way to explain everything to Maggie so that she wouldn't leave me for good. Nervous, I kneaded the scar on my right hand.

"You say I left you seven years ago," I explained. "But for me, it was only a few days ago."

Maggie stared at me, unblinking.

I continued, "I skipped from 2009 to 2016. But I don't know how."

"I've heard some inventive excuses for guys ghosting me, but this one is top notch!" Maggie snapped. "That's a new one. Why don't you tell me that you didn't want to date me anymore? I'm a big girl. I can handle it." She glanced over at the clock on the wall. "The clock is ticking."

"Maggie, it's the truth, I swear," I blurted. "Somehow I'm traveling in time. Prashant and I did an experiment in his chemistry lab and it exploded and knocked me on my ass. I blacked out. Then a couple of days later, a street light shattered over my head. I think the two things reacted with my internal ions, because ever since then, I've jumped to different time frames in my life."

"You expect me to believe this?" Maggie scoffed. "You obviously need some serious help. Maybe get some Xanax or something."

"Yes, I want you to believe me," I begged. "I have never lied to you and I'm not about to start now."

"Then prove it to me," she replied, with a faint wave of her hand.

"Okay," I said. My mind scurried, trying to think of something. "Do you remember the first time you met your ex-husband?"

"Yeah, I met Brett at a party at CMU," Maggie recalled. "With you. But he and I didn't start dating until a few years later. What does that have to do with you?"

"Because if it wasn't for me traveling in time and going back to that party, you would never have met him," I expressed. "In my original present, you married someone else."

"What? That doesn't even make any sense." Maggie shook her head at me.

"Oh, right." I slapped myself in the forehead. "Your whole life trajectory changed but you didn't realize it changed."

"Ryan, this better get good real soon, or I'm leaving in a few minutes."

"I promise you it will. Then while you were at Penn, you met Tamara," I explained.

"Yeah, I remember you coming to Boston and meeting her," Maggie added.

"Whatever happened to her?" I inquired. "Do you two still talk?"

Maggie sighed like a soft, deflated balloon. "No. Tamara was killed by a drunk driver on her way to work in October, 1995. I was devastated. I couldn't get out of bed for a week."

"Holy shit." Maggie's raw feelings left me breathless.

His Second Chance

"It was a long time ago," Maggie said, her voice barely audible. "I had a tough time getting over her death. I really loved her."

That explained how Maggie hadn't dated any women since.

Maggie continued, "Then I met Brett again a year later. He happened to also be working in Boston at the same time. He came up to me at a coffee shop and said, 'Have we met before?' I thought it was some dumb pickup line, but we soon discovered that yes, we had met before. Brett was kind and helped me get out of my funk after Tamara died. I fought my feelings for him for the longest time because I believed I wanted to be exclusively with women. Then Brett and I eventually fell in love, got married, and had Madelyn and Thomas." Maggie narrowed her brows at me, realizing she overstepped. "Wait, you were supposed to explain everything to me. Not the other way around."

"I'm sorry, I was so caught up in your story that I let you talk," I answered. "After I met Tamara with you, I went to Pittsburgh in 1998. It was a repeat of me getting my Masters at CMU. I encountered Prashant again. And Randy Pausch."

"The *Last Lecture* guy?" Maggie asked.

"Yes, this was well before he met his future wife and was diagnosed with cancer," I explained. "He helped me resurrect a dead butterfly. And it was my fault. I was such a dumbass."

Maggie laughed out loud. Her expression was a positive change from moments earlier.

"After that, I jumped back to Boston in 2003."

"I don't remember seeing you then," Maggie acknowledged.

"You didn't," I confessed.

His Second Chance

"Then how can you prove to me that you were there?" she asked. "What if you're making all of this up to get me to believe you?"

"I swear I'm not," I insisted. "When I saw you in Boston, you were taking your kids to school. Madelyn must have been heading to kindergarten or something because she had a purple unicorn backpack. And Thomas was collecting rocks and you stopped him to zip up his jacket."

"Oh yeah, I remember that day," Maggie recalled. "It was windy and Thomas wanted to keep all of the rocks in his pocket."

"Then Mav—I mean Brett, came running after you with your coffee," I continued. "He had a little brown and white dog on a leash who wore a blue vest."

"Rocky," Maggie added with a wistful gaze in her eyes. "He was a good dog. The kids adored him."

"I didn't want to talk to you then because I witnessed how happy you were and I didn't want to infringe on that. I would never forgive myself if I messed up your life."

Maggie stared at me with suspicious eyes. "You're saying all this, but it doesn't prove you traveled in time. It only proves that you were on that corner on that date. Stalking me." She eyed the clock on the wall again.

"True." I lowered my head in shame. "But I wasn't stalking you. I swear."

"Then prove to me that you traveled in time," Maggie ordered. "Tell me something that will happen in the future."

His Second Chance

I gazed around the restaurant trying to come up with something. My focus settled on a group of men in dark blue suits at the bar, some D.C. politicians grabbing a few drinks after work.

"The presidential election is coming up on Tuesday, right?" I stated.

"Yeah, why?"

"As much as I hate to say it, Donald Trump will win," I replied. "And then he'll be impeached in 2019."

"What?!" Maggie shouted. "That guy is a big, orange buffoon. No wonder he gets impeached."

"It's true," I told her. "As much as I hate that I know it, it's true. And Hillary will take some time to give him her concessional phone call because she didn't have a speech ready."

"Because she can't believe it herself," Maggie chuckled.

"Not only that, he loses re-election, and two weeks before the end of his term, he incites a riot to storm the US Capitol because he claims the election was stolen from him. So he was impeached a second time. He never concedes and refuses to go the inauguration."

"What a sore loser," Maggie scoffed. "I know some little kids who behave better than that."

"I know." I nodded.

"Even though this sucks about our government, I'll know you'll prove to me if you're telling the truth."

HIS SECOND CHANCE

Chapter 34

I glanced at the clock on the wall.

"My ten minutes are up," I said. "Do you still wanna bolt?"

Maggie blew out another sigh. "I can't."

"What do you mean you can't?" I asked. "You mean you don't want to or you physically can't?"

"I physically can't," Maggie replied.

She reached below the table and pulled out a purple walking cane. My mouth fell open in an O.

"What—Why do you have that?" I begged the question.

"Because," Maggie explained, "I was in a terrible car accident six months ago and I fractured my back in three places. My doctor couldn't predict if I would ever walk again."

"Oh my god," was all I could manage to say. How could this happen and I not be aware of it? My sweet Maggie was hurt and I couldn't do anything about it. I wished I could have jumped back six months earlier to prevent it. Now she had to walk with a cane. No wonder she struggled to get out of the booth. My heart broke. I almost lost her.

"But now I'm not only walking, but also driving." Maggie beamed with pride. "Something the doc didn't expect me to do for at least a year."

"You're amazing," I gushed. "So strong and inspiring."

"Thank you," Maggie replied. "Thomas has been a big help since he's home with me. He carries my laundry, he drove me around before I was cleared to drive, and he gets things out of the high cabinets so that I don't fall off a stool."

"Everything a fine son should do," I added.

"Yeah, he is," Maggie gushed. "I couldn't ask for a better one."

"And Madelyn?"

"She's fantastic, too," Maggie replied. "I know I'm biased, but I have some pretty great kids."

"You are lucky in more ways than one," I said.

"Listen, if you *think* you'll be around tomorrow, you know with your time traveling and all, would you like to have dinner with Thomas and me?" Maggie joked with me.

At least she started to believe me.

"Yes, I would love that," I chimed.

"Good," she replied. "But wait, you never told me *how* you travel in time. I mean come on, that's pretty far-fetched. It's not like you're in a magical DeLorean or anything."

"I'm still trying to figure that out," I stated. "All I know is I fall asleep in one time period and wake up in another. Like I said, I think it has something to do with the lab explosion and the street

HIS SECOND CHANCE

light shattering above me. It's screwing with my molecular structure. Do you remember the moment when I asked you to wait for me on New Year's Eve?"

"Yes. How could I forget?"

"I figured the jumping feeling came on because of the fireworks above us," I replied. "That was the only time that I've been able to foresee it."

"Do you think you are at the mercy of forever traveling in time?" Maggie begged the question. "Like in *Quantum Leap*?"

"I don't know," I pondered. "I hope not. I want to stay with you—if you'll have me."

"I guess that depends on your prophecy for the election on Tuesday!" Maggie joked.

I barked a laugh. Maggie never ceased to make me smile.

* * * *

After spending the night in a hotel room by myself, I took the Metro to get to Maggie's house the next day. She lived in Anacostia, across the river from the Navy Yard. After walking 10 minutes from the Metro station, I headed up the hill to Maggie's home. She lived in a tall and narrow, hill-top Victorian settled on a postage stamp yard. What the cute yellow house lacked in grass, it made up for in height.

I jogged up the three steps to her front porch and rapped on the front door.

223

His Second Chance

A few moments later, a tall and thin teenage boy answered the door. He wore a wrinkled, gray, Georgetown T-shirt and wrinkled jeans. His shaggy, dark hair wisped into small curls above his ears. Reminded me a lot of myself when I was his age.

"Hi, you must be Ryan," he said to me.

"Yes, and you must be Thomas," I replied.

Thomas nodded. "My mom said to bring you into the kitchen. She's making paella. Come on in."

I followed Thomas through the living room and dining room and into the kitchen. Maggie hovered at the stove, a cloud of steam rising above her. She turned when we walked into the room and hobbled over to us. Her cane suctioned in beats on the hardwood floor as she slowly took each step. My heart sank as I watched her. I should have been there to prevent the car accident.

"Hi! So glad you could come," she said. "Dinner will be ready in about five minutes. What can we get you to drink?"

"What do you have?" I asked.

Thomas opened the refrigerator door and stuck his head in. "We have lemonade, iced tea, Coke, Red Bull, and Gatorade."

"I'll take a Red Bull," I answered. "With ice if you don't mind."

"Sure thing," Thomas replied.

I spoke to Maggie as I followed her back to the stove, "You have a good kid there."

"I like to think so," she gushed. "When he goes to college, I'll be alone for the first time since I finished undergrad. I don't know what I'm going to do with myself."

"Well, maybe I can remedy that." I winked at her.

His Second Chance

Maggie grinned widely at me. "Maybe." She pointed to a cabinet across the kitchen. "Can you grab three dinner plates for us? The silverware is in the drawer directly below."

"Yes, of course," I said.

For the next two hours, Maggie, Thomas, and I shared good food and good conversation. Thomas and I bantered over who was the best player on the Nationals, while Maggie was more interested in the Caps. We also discussed art and current events. Thomas disclosed his plans to apply to Virginia Tech. Being with them warmed my insides and I didn't want the feeling to end. They made me believe this was where I belonged.

As I left Maggie's house and headed back to the Metro station, a street light exploded across the hushed street.

Damn.

His Second Chance

Chapter 35

"Is he dead?" Taj said near my ear as I lay motionless on the couch.

"I don't know," Gia answered. "If not, he's been sleeping for a long time. Like Sleeping Beauty."

"But he's no beauty. More like a beast." Taj barked a laugh at his own joke.

Seconds later, a couple sets of small fingers poked at my cheeks and nose, trying to elicit a reaction.

Without a sound, nor opening my eyes, I reached and grabbed their tiny fingers in my hands. Taj and Gia shrieked with laughter as I pulled them close to me into a hug.

"You can't slip anything past your Uncle Ryan," I finally spoke with open eyes.

"Do you want to come outside and play with us?" Gia pleaded. Her long dark hair and dark skin matched her mother's. She wore a light blue T-shirt that said "Girls Rule" in thick, gold lettering.

HIS SECOND CHANCE

"We're gonna ride our bikes down to the park," Taj added. He wore a black T-shirt with the words "Beast Mode" emblazoned on the front. "You can ride my dad's."

I wriggled my way off the couch and the kids made room for me to stand in front of them. "Let me find out if your parents want me to do anything first," I said. "If not, I'd love to."

Taj and Gia scurried into the kitchen and I followed them. I found Prashant and Manju sitting at the kitchen table with an open laptop in front of them. Taj and Gia then busied themselves with a tablet.

"Look who's up and moving around," Manju joked.

I rubbed my forehead as if I had slept for days. "What time is it?"

"Just after 11:00," Manju replied.

"How's your head?" Prashant asked. "You had a bad fall yesterday. I still think you should see a doctor."

Yesterday?

I was back in the present. Back in Prashant and Manju's house. Back with Taj and Gia and their toys strewn everywhere. Life was good.

"Either I had the weirdest dream," I joked, "or you two will not believe what happened to me."

"Why? What happened?" Manju shut the laptop and focused her attention on me. I took a seat at the table next to Prashant.

I stared at Prashant for nonverbal assistance. Convincing him was hard the first time. Hopefully Manju would believe me as well.

His Second Chance

"Honey," Prashant said to Manju, "we have something to tell you." Then he glared at me and wiped a hand along his chin stubble. "Go ahead, Ryan, tell her."

"You two are being weird," she pointed out. "Weirder than normal."

"I'm not sure how it's happening, but I'm pretty certain I can travel back in time," I blurted.

Manju howled in laughter. "Oh, come on," she put a hand to her belly. "You expect me to believe you?"

I exchanged glances with Prashant, before answering Manju. "Yes."

"Nobody travels in time," she insisted. "If they could, we would have had a cure for so many diseases. Or 9/11 might not have happened."

"But it's true," Prashant backed me up. "I even helped him try to get back to where he needed to be."

Manju laughed again then glanced around the room as if she was searching for hidden cameras. "Is this payback for me pranking you on April Fool's Day last year?"

"No, I swear." I held my hand up like a stop signal. "I'm not making this up."

"Babe, he's telling the truth," Prashant added.

Manju finally stopped laughing and glared at us with a furrowed brow. I could sense the doubt leaving her like heat off a radiator. "So, you're like Marty McFly in *Back to the Future*?"

"Yes, but without the DeLorean," I answered.

His Second Chance

"What did you do?" Manju's skepticism echoed in her voice. "What happened at the lab yesterday? You two are the smartest guys I know. If you can replicate and control this, the science community will never be the same. Hell, *history* will never be the same."

I pondered about how I almost fucked up Prashant and Manju's relationship. Telling someone too much about their possible life trajectories could mess them up. "That's why we can't tell anyone about this."

"But you could win a Nobel Prize!" Manju offered.

"I'm willing to give that up," I replied.

Prashant interrupted, "Something happened at the lab when I tried to create a new lithium ion battery. I screwed up the calculations and the whole thing exploded."

"And knocked me out," I added.

"Then what happened?" Manju wanted to know.

"I actually already started this day once before," I explained. "A couple times, actually." I glanced around Prashant and Manju's kitchen. Their kids were still engulfed with playing on their tablets. Something was missing. "But the first time I was here, you had a large print of the Hyderabad temples on the wall."

Manju's mouth fell open into an O. "Taj played ball in the house last week and knocked it off the wall and broke it."

I continued, "That day, I offered to go to Hemingway's to get burgers and fries. As I left the bar, a street light on Forbes Avenue exploded on top of me."

229

His Second Chance

"We think that's what triggers his jumps," Prashant added. "The combination of the two types of explosions is mixing with his molecular chemistry."

"But not always," I remarked. "The one time I stayed in 2009 for close to a month. And that was the only time that I had a premonition that I would jump again."

"Why? What happened then?" Manju questioned.

"New Year's Eve fireworks," I explained. "Every other time I jumped, something randomly exploded that I couldn't predict coming. A street light. A neon beer sign at PHI."

"PHI?" Manju raised an eyebrow. "That's where Prashant and I met in 1999."

"Yes, that was one of my jumps," I replied. I couldn't tell her that it was my fault that she and Prashant might not have gotten together. Nor could I tell Prashant that Manju was first interested in me. He would never forgive me. Fortunately for all of us, it all worked out for them.

"Is there any continuity to all of your jumps?" Prashant questioned. He pushed his sleeves up and revealed the black tattoo on his forearm. I envisioned his brain churning trying to figure everything out. He might not want the world to be aware of his explosion, but he needed answers for himself.

I shook my head. "The only thing I know is that I jump to insignificant times in my life or someone else's. I've been back and forth to CMU a few times, in Boston twice to see Maggie—"

"Maggie who? Kevin's sister Maggie?" Manju challenged. "Wait, weren't you with that girl Rebecca for a while?"

His Second Chance

Mental head slap. That's right. Manju and Maggie never met. Manju only heard about Maggie through Kevin. In the previous present, I mused about Maggie only to myself and accepted the fact that I would never be with her. Now that I had altered the course of Maggie's life and mine, she and I had a chance to be together. But every time I jumped, Manju and Maggie never crossed paths.

"Yes, Kevin's sister Maggie," Prashant spoke for me. "The numbnut's been in love with her since the day he met her and he never told her. So now he has a second chance."

"That's right," I mused. "She's the love of my life. I finally told her I loved her. Long story short, she and I can hopefully be together. As long as I can figure out how to control the time traveling."

"Where and when did you last see her?" Manju asked.

HIS SECOND CHANCE

Chapter 36

"November 5, 2016," I said. "A few days before the election."

"How'd you leave it with her?" Prashant asked.

"She, like you," I motioned to both of them, "thought I was fucking with her when I told her I traveled in time. But I'm pretty sure I convinced her when I told her Trump would get elected president."

"No one predicted that." Manju rolled her eyes and huffed.

I continued, "The last time I saw Maggie, I had dinner with her and her teenage son Thomas. Great kid, by the way. When I left her house that night, a street lamp exploded on the way back to my hotel. To me, that was yesterday." I pursed my lips together as I glanced around their kitchen. "And now I'm here."

"And you want to go back to her?" Manju asked. The corners of her mouth formed into a soft curl. As smart-ass as she was, Manju believed in me finding love.

"Yes," I replied. "Maggie's the love of my life. I never want to be without her again. She makes me feel whole. I fucked it up the first

His Second Chance

time with her and I won't let it happen again." I glared at them with pleading eyes. "You have to help me stay with her."

"Let's think this through." Prashant's gaze ricocheted around the room as his brain churned. "Since it's now the present, you don't want to jump again, correct?"

"Right," I said. "Is there any way to prevent it from happening again?"

"We'd need to figure out how you're jumping and prevent it," Prashant explained. "We already have proof that the lab blast and lights are factors..."

"But now that I think about it," I recalled, "there were a few times where a light exploded around me and I *didn't* jump. In D.C. and in Baltimore in 2009."

"What was the variable?" Prashant wanted to know.

"I have no idea." I shook my head.

"You had to have done something different to make you not jump," Manju added.

"I don't know what it would be," I said. "I lived with Rebecca then. Every other jump I was single."

"True, but I doubt your relationship status affected your molecular structure," Prashant pointed out.

"I had my car then too," I offered. "Every other time I either traveled by train, walked, or took your car."

Prashant shook his head in refute. "Again, won't affect your makeup."

"Did you eat anything different?" Manju added. "Maybe that had something to do with it?"

233

His Second Chance

"Among other things, I had tacos in Pittsburgh, oysters in Boston, Mediterranean food in D.C., and crabs in Baltimore," I recalled.

"You're quite the foodie," Manju joked.

"Everything sounds pretty normal," Prashant deduced.

"What about drinks?" Manju asked.

"Beers, wine, bourbon, the usual stuff," I answered.

Then it hit me. I slapped myself in the forehead. "I'm such a dumbass."

"What?" Prashant and Manju exclaimed in unison.

"When I was in D.C. and dating Rebecca, she told me that my doctor told me to limit my caffeine."

"Yeah, so?" Manju replied.

"Prashant, what did we drink a ton of in the lab *yesterday*?" I asked him, already knowing the answer.

"Red Bull," he replied. "I picked up a dozen empty cans off the floor after you left in the Uber."

"There are over a hundred milligrams of caffeine in those drinks!" Manju reprimanded us. "You two will be bouncing off the walls for days!"

"Believe me, I know," I added. "It's what got me through grad school. Anyway, I didn't drink anything like that the entire time I was in 2009, until ..." my voice trailed, when I realized I could have prevented jumping on the best night of my life.

"Until what?" Prashant questioned.

"Until New Year's Eve," I recalled. "When I told Maggie I loved her. I wanted to stay awake that night so I drank some Red Bull.

His Second Chance

And that's when the fireworks went off at midnight and caused me to jump again."

"Duh. There's your answer," Manju assessed. "The combination of the lab blast, any light or fireworks exploding near you, and the high caffeine in those energy drinks."

"I can't do anything about the lab explosion or lights," I added, "but I won't drink any more Red Bulls or Monster Energy drinks. I can't leave Maggie again. I want to be with her for the rest of my life. She can't slip away from me again. I want to marry her."

"Where is she now?" Prashant asked.

"I assume she's still living in D.C.," I replied.

"Only one way to find out," Manju added. She opened the laptop on the table in front of us and pushed it in toward me.

I logged into my Facebook account, found Maggie's account, and smiled wide. "She's still in D.C."

Prashant and Manju exchanged glances as if they shared an inside joke.

"Go get her," Prashant stated with a broad grin.

Manju stood from the table, leaned over, and hugged me. "I can't wait to hear what happens." She turned and left Prashant and me alone in the kitchen. Taj and Gia trailed her into the hallway.

I nervously bit my lip.

"What's wrong?" Prashant asked.

"Let's hope that these three things are what causes me to travel in time," I began. "But what if it's something else? Something else we're not thinking of."

"I suppose it's possible," Prashant replied.

His Second Chance

"If that's the case, and I jump," I said, "I might not see you again."

"Don't say that," Prashant stated. "You'll be fine. You always are."

"But in case I'm not, I want to tell you I love you, man. You're my best friend." I embraced Prashant and held tight, fearful that we might not cross paths again. I didn't want to leave him, but I knew I had to. "I don't know what I'd do without you."

Prashant smiled. "I'll see you on the other side, brother. Go get her."

HIS SECOND CHANCE

Chapter 37

A half hour later, I was in my rental car on my way to Washington, D.C. again. My mind wandered as I weaved in and out of traffic on The Parkway East heading toward the Pennsylvania Turnpike. In Maggie's lifetime, she hadn't seen me in five years. The last time I showed up in her life, she gave me a tongue lashing for ghosting her. I liked to think that this time could be different. Maybe she'd go nuts and jump into my arms and wrap her legs around my waist and make out with me like on an episode of *The Bachelor*?

Or she might slap me in the face for abandoning her again. I prepared myself for anything.

I didn't give Maggie any warning that I was on my way to visit her. A mixture of excitement and nervousness overwhelmed me. I couldn't wait to tell Maggie that I wanted to spend the rest of my life with her. But what if she changed her mind? What if she didn't want to ever face me because I left her yet again? What if she was so angry with me that she couldn't forgive me?

237

His Second Chance

A few hours later, I parked on Maggie's street in Anacostia. Several cars and SUVs lined both sides of the narrow street—residents' since none of the houses had driveways. A few kids played in the green yards, squealing at each other. I exited my car and shuffled along the red brick sidewalk toward Maggie's house. Her homestead was quiet now that Madelyn and Thomas were both out of the house.

I scampered up the sidewalk and four steps that led to Maggie's front porch. I rapped on her door and waited. No answer. I knocked on the door a second time. Again, no answer. God, I was such a dumbass. I didn't even think that she might not be home.

Defeated, I turned and trudged back to my car. I had no idea where to find her. She could be anywhere. The grocery store. Work. Visiting friends. Out of town for the weekend.

"Miss Maggie is in her backyard," a curious neighborhood youngster called to me from an adjacent yard.

"Thanks, buddy." I waved to him and trotted off Maggie's front porch. Turning the corner of the house and easing through the narrow side yard, I found Maggie facing away from me, kneeling in front of a decimated flower bed. A plastic flat of pristine colorful blossoms lay next to her in the grass, ready to be planted.

"Do you want some help with them?" I spoke from behind her.

Startled, Maggie whipped around and faced me. Wow, she still looked good. Even though a few rogue pieces of dirt speckled her face, she was the most beautiful woman I had ever laid eyes on. She wore a red Capitals T-shirt and black jersey shorts.

"Ryan!" Maggie blurted. "What are you doing here?"

His Second Chance

"I came to see you." I took a step closer to her, closing the gap between us.

She tugged the garden gloves from her hands, tossed them on the ground next to her, and stood up to face me. Her swift movements made me think that her body had fully recovered from her car accident. "Wow, what a surprise." Maggie leaned into me and hugged me. Relieved that she was happy to see me, I pulled her close to me, touching every part of her body with mine.

"You look stunning," I whispered in her ear. "It should be a crime how cute you are."

Maggie chuckled, embarrassed that she was dirty, sweaty, and not looking her best.

I released Maggie and held her in front of me. "No, I mean it. You are the most beautiful woman I have ever met."

Turning the color of her T-shirt, Maggie sheepishly smiled and gazed downward.

I took Maggie's hands in mine and smiled at her. She made me want to be a better man. Without another thought, I knelt in front of her. "Maggie, you are the love of my life and I never want to be without you again. Falling in love with you was the easy part. Admitting it to myself was a little more difficult. It took crossing so many lifetimes to realize that you are the one for me. Will you marry me?"

"What ..." Maggie released my hands and stepped backwards. Her face twisted into deep annoyance. "No ... no ..."

"Because you're with someone else?" The notion didn't dawn on me until now. I was such a dumbass. Of course, she was dating

His Second Chance

someone. She was a catch. I didn't even think that she might say no. I stood upright in front of her.

"What? No, that's not it," Maggie answered. "I'm not seeing anyone."

A sigh of relief escaped my lips. Total embarrassment averted. "Then why no?"

"Because," Maggie explained, "you can't show up here five years later and propose to me. That's not how it works."

"But I love you," I blurted. "I've always loved you."

"And I've always loved you, too," Maggie replied. "But how do I have proof that you won't disappear on me again? You've been gone for five years. That's not fair to me if you leave me again."

"Because I finally figured out how I traveled in time," I spouted. "Well, Prashant and his wife and I did. So, I'm not going anywhere ever again. I promise you that."

"How did you figure it out?" Maggie eyed me suspiciously.

"Prashant, Manju, and I sat at their kitchen table and we pieced it all together," I began. "Remember how I told you that the lab accident and light explosions caused me to jump?"

"Yes."

"Well, it wasn't only that," I said. "It was also every time I drank a Red Bull or Monster Energy drink. The high caffeine content mixed with the chemical reaction inside me from the lab and the light explosions caused me to travel in time. I can't control when a light explodes again, but I can stop drinking Red Bull. It's an easy sacrifice to guarantee that I will never leave you again."

"Never?" Maggie arched a mischievous eyebrow at me.

His Second Chance

"Never." My heart skipped a beat. Her gorgeous smile made me whole. I loved her with every ounce of my being. "Do you believe me?"

"Yes," she chuckled. "I just wanted you to tell me that it won't happen again because I don't know how much more I can take. Ever since the 2016 election I realized you were telling the truth. And I've waited for you to show up again. I couldn't predict when, but I knew you would."

I pulled Maggie close to me again, wrapping my arms around her. "I promise you I will never leave you again." Cupping her chin in my hands, I kissed her soft lips. "I'm asking you again."

I broke the embrace and knelt in front of Maggie a second time, taking her hands in mine. She beamed at me and I was pretty confident of the answer. "Maggie, you are the love of my life. You make me so happy. You make my problems seem more manageable. Every time I'm with you, I can't stop smiling. I love that I can open up to you and you make me feel so comfortable. I've never felt that with anyone else. I never want to be without you. We were meant to meet. If there were past lives, we scorched the Earth in a previous one. I love you with every atom in my body. Will you be my wife so that I can love you for the rest of my life?"

"Yes!" Maggie shrieked. "Yes! Yes! You are the love of my life. I don't want to spend any more time without you."

I quickly stood up and Maggie jumped into my arms, wrapping her legs around me. She planted one of her trademark heart-stopping kisses on my lips. I could kiss her soft, warm lips for hours. I never wanted to be with another woman.

His Second Chance

The world fell away that Maggie would be mine forever.

HIS SECOND CHANCE

Chapter 38

Many, many years later

As I settled on the back porch swing, my old bones creaked and ached. They served me well over the years and I was thankful to get around as well as I could, even with the occasional use of a cane. Even after all these years, the scar on my right hand remained, interwoven between deep creases that came with age. My mind still believed a young man resided in me, but my lack of hair, a hunched back, and earned wrinkles of life proved otherwise. I didn't walk or react as fast as I used to, but I enjoyed every day life presented me.

In the lush, green yard, my great-grandson plucked a few rocks out of the bedding of a sycamore tree. He reminded me of another young boy I watched do that several decades earlier. The blonde four-year-old in front of me shoved the rocks in his pockets and skipped toward me, tripping over his small, wobbly legs.

His Second Chance

"Boys, dinner will be ready in ten minutes," an aging female voice called from inside the house. That voice belonged to the love of my life. She helped me find my glasses and I held her arm as she walked down the stairs. Marrying her was the best decision I ever made. Every birthday, Valentine's Day, and anniversary, I secretly went to the post office and sent her a card in the mail so that she knew how much I adored her. I clutched her hand whenever I could, securing the promise that I would never leave her. As an internal promise, I never drank another Red Bull.

"Okay, Maggie," I answered her through the open window. "We'll be in soon."

Even though Maggie and I didn't have children together, I took Madelyn and Thomas as my own. They both married and gave us a handful of grandchildren. The little guy in front of me was our first great-grandchild.

He climbed up the porch steps, taking one at a time with his tiny legs. Once he reached the top, he shuffled over to me and tried to climb on my lap. I reached down to him and slowly pulled him the rest of the way up. The aches in my limbs were worth spending time with him.

"There ya go," I said. As he settled on my lap, I tousled his wavy blonde hair.

He gazed up at me with wide, green eyes. Those eyes. Eyes he inherited from his wonderful great-grandmother.

"Great-Grampa, tell me a story," he begged.

"Sure, Little Ryan," I told my namesake. "Do I have a story for you ..."

His Second Chance

The End

His Second Chance

His Second Chance

Thank you for reading my book.
If you enjoyed it, won't you please take a moment to leave me a review at your favorite retailer?
One or two sentences are perfectly fine.
Help an author out. ☺
Thanks!

Want some cool merch from me?
Post a pic of this book on your social media and tag me!
@marywalshwrites

Tag me on:

    BB aℕauthor

Sign up for my sometimes-monthly newsletter and order autographed books at:
marywalshwrites.com

Follow me on Goodreads and Amazon:
www.goodreads.com/goodreadscommarywalshwrites
www.amazon.com/author/marywalsh2

Printed in the USA
CPSIA information can be obtained
at www.ICGtesting.com
LVHW021811290524
781190LV00033B/181